Sign up for our newsletter to hear
about new and upcoming releases.

www.ylva-publishing.com

IF LOOKS COULD KILL

ANDI MARQUETTE

 THE LAW GAME - BOOK 5

CHAPTER 1

"Here's the target."

Ellie took the folder and opened it. A photo was fastened to the inside cover, and the woman in it stared out at her, almost glaring. "Wait." She looked up at him. "This is Marya Hampstead."

"Yep." Rick took his suit jacket off and slung it over the back of the chair at his own desk. He rolled his shirt sleeves up, something he did when he was in the office, and straightened his tie. Rick was built like a prize fighter, and Ellie figured he had his shirts custom-made to accommodate his musculature. A long scar marred the underside of his left forearm, pinkish against the brown of his skin, a souvenir of his service in Afghanistan.

"*The* Marya Hampstead," she said. "Fashion mogul. Bitch on wheels." And ultra-hot, she finished to herself. Seemed beauty was wasted on people like her.

He clicked the remote and brought up Marya's portfolio on the big screen that hung near his desk. Hampstead glared out at him now, too. "You're quick, Els. Guess that's why you're part of this unit of NYPD." He flashed her a grin.

She ignored the ribbing and rolled her chair over to his desk. "What's the deal?"

He clicked to another photo that showed Hampstead with a well-dressed man, entering a restaurant. She had her hand on his arm. "That's Lyev Koslov," Rick said.

"Looks familiar. Is he part of the Koslov family here?"

"Yep. The Koslovs might be tied in with international arms dealers overseas."

"Define 'tied in.'"

"Daddy Koslov—the head honcho—runs a company in Moscow that makes medical equipment. However, a couple of his shipments were intercepted in Turkey. The shit in the boxes was not scalpels or clamps." He clicked to another photo that showed military-grade rifles and ammo.

"Where were they headed?"

"Yemen."

Which was currently a hotbed of crazy, with layers of civil war, violence, and whatever other atrocities people dealt out to each other.

"There are complicating factors."

Of course there were. "Which are what, exactly?"

Rick put another photo on his screen. It showed a dead guy, a standard autopsy photo that featured him from the pecs up; the stitched-up Y-cut on his chest was visible just above the sheet. A small black hole was positioned almost perfectly in the center of his forehead.

"And who's this poor soul?" she asked.

"One of the Petrovs, but not of the New York Petrovs, though he is related. A second cousin of the boss here in the city. This dude was based in Moscow up until this past January. Then he wasn't based on this earth at all."

"Professional hit," she said, leaning forward a bit. He looked like he was in his early thirties. "Not very old."

"Thirty-two. Not married, and somewhat of a playboy." Rick clicked the mouse and an autopsy photo of another dead guy showed up.

2

"Also execution."

"This is another Petrov," Rick said. "Also cousin to Boss Petrov."

"Call me crazy, but I'm sensing a pattern."

"Damn, you're really quick," he said with a little smile. "This gentleman was found in Prague about two months after the first died." Rick pulled up a third autopsy photo. "Comes in threes, for now." One more Russian guy, shot execution style. "This is yet another Petrov. His mother is a first cousin to Boss Petrov, and she's originally from St. Petersburg. She married a Brit and still lives in London. His body was found there in June."

"Okay, so it looks like the same hit man did all three. What ties them together besides the Petrov connection?"

Rick clicked his mouse again, and a photo of a local boss filled the screen, wearing an expensive suit, sunglasses, and standing outside one of the restaurants he owned in the city. He was in his mid-sixties, but he maintained himself, and he was always in the company of younger women, though he did have a wife.

"The Petrovs are also involved in arms dealings," Rick said, sounding like a college professor. "We've been following this guy for a couple of years now. He's on Interpol's radar, too, but he's pretty slick. All three dead dudes were involved in Petrov gun-running, though they managed to keep their hands clean. They arranged sales, apparently, serving as the middlemen between buyer and seller, but never got caught with anything."

"So they were points of contact." Ellie rolled her chair back to her desk, grabbed her coffee cup, and rolled right back to Rick's.

"Most likely. And probably helped organize meetings and networking. So law enforcement overseas wasn't able to make much stick. And then they turned up dead."

Ellie sipped. "So what does any of this have to do with Lyev Koslov and Hampstead?"

Rick pulled the photo of Marya and Lyev up again. "We think there's some kind of private territorial war going on between the Koslovs and the Petrovs."

"An arms race, basically." Figures. Any time there were guns and money to be made, people got greedy. And violent.

"Something like that. The thing is, the Koslovs don't have a history in arms dealing, and Daddy Koslov insists his family isn't involved, and he insists that he has no beef with the Petrovs."

"But the Petrovs are blaming him for the murders."

"Yep." Rick took a sip of his diet soda.

"What about the guns that turned up in Koslov's medical supply boxes in Turkey?"

He screwed the top back on the bottle and set it down. "Koslov claims he was set up, that those boxes were stolen from the supply warehouse in Russia. He's got a police report to prove it."

Ellie snorted. "Easy to fake that."

"Yeah. Except Koslov seems worried. He's wondering if somebody in the family has gone rogue and has personal beef with the Petrovs. He's running tons of diplomacy right now with Boss Petrov, and word on the street is Petrov is giving Koslov time to see if that's the case."

"Could be Petrov is popping his own guys to set Koslov up to take a fall. Koslov's empire is bigger than Petrov's, and he's been at the game longer." All this underground mob stuff could get really shitty like that.

"We thought about that, too. But Petrov personally worked with the men who died, and from what we can glean, they were good at their jobs. No mob guy is going to get rid of assets like that to make a point or set a trap."

Ellie frowned. "Okay, so basically, we want to know if Big Daddy Koslov is lying about arms dealing. If he's not, then we want to know if maybe Lyev is doing it or if somebody else is, and using Big Daddy's various businesses as fronts and killing off Petrovs because he wants their markets."

"Nailed it. The last thing anybody wants is a mob war between two powerful Russian families like this, especially when it's so damn easy to get guns up the I-95 corridor. They could flood the city with them."

"That's such a lovely thought, Rick. Thank you. As if we're not already inundated with assholes."

He laughed, and Ellie looked at the photo of Marya and Lyev on the big screen again. "So what the hell does Marya Hampstead have to do with this?"

"We don't know. We're trying to figure that out. We're also trying to figure out what Hampstead's relationship to Lyev Koslov is. And what he's up to with her."

"When was this picture taken?"

"Almost two months ago."

Ellie frowned, skeptical. "The guy's a businessman. She's a businesswoman. Her dad does international banking in the UK. These two probably met at a party or some dinner or something and had a fling. That's how they do it in those circles."

"Totally possible. Except Daddy Hampstead spends a lot of time with Koslov holdings overseas, and we're not sure what he's up to. He's been spotted in Moscow, cozying up to former KGB."

"Practically everybody in the Kremlin is former KGB, including Putin." Ellie rolled her chair back to her desk and took one of her cinnamon Jolly Ranchers out of a drawer. She unwrapped it and put it in her mouth. "Businesses over there are probably full of ex-KGB, too," she said around the candy as its spicy kick filled her mouth.

"True. But Jonathan Hampstead has ready access to all kinds of international contacts, and he'd be able to get the money to help broker a few arms deals." Rick sipped his soda again.

"So we're targeting her to get to Daddy Hampstead." Her tongue burned a little from the cinnamon.

"And Lyev Koslov."

"Even though she hasn't been seen with him for almost two months."

"But he might be hanging out with her dad, still." Rick gave her a look over his shoulder.

"And what about Jonathan Hampstead? Maybe he's taking care of all the Petrovs."

Rick studied her. "That thought has crossed my mind, but there is zero evidence to support it."

"Seriously?" Ellie raised her eyebrows. "Assassins-R-Us on the deep web. Burn phone. Meeting, payment, done."

"Again, we have zero evidence for any of that. And he's an international businessman making money hand over fist. He doesn't need to run arms."

"No, but people still do it, no matter how much money they make legitimately."

Rick shook his head. "We've got no evidence, Els. So let's stick with what we know."

"Fine. Rain on my damn parade. When was the last time Marya saw Dad?"

"A month ago in London. He's British and based there. Plus, she has fashion shit she has to do all the time over there and in Paris. His ex-wife—Marya's mom—is Greek. The ex still lives in London, too, and it seems she's still cordial with dad and daughter. Marya is a British citizen, but like a lot of international business-types, that hasn't been a roadblock to running Fashion Forward and living here. Read the file and see if you can fill in some holes." He pointed at the screen. "We're starting this op in about a week. By that time, you'd better know Hampstead's favorite music, what wine she likes, and the kind of toilet paper she uses."

Ellie raised her eyebrows. "C'mon," she said. "People that rich pay others to wipe their asses."

He laughed. "Then find out what the servants buy."

Ellie took a drink of cold coffee. "So how is this going to go down?"

"We're putting someone inside."

"Inside what?"

"Hampstead's outfit. Fashion Forward publications."

Ellie nodded, approving. "Ambitious. Who gets that job?"

He grinned at her, like a shark.

She stared at him. "Oh, no. Hell, no. I know nothing about that shit."

"Don't worry. We'll get you ready." At her expression, he picked a piece of paper up from his desk and handed it to her. "Hampstead is looking for an intern."

Ellie didn't read it. "No. I'm too old." And she really hated everything to do with the world of fashion.

"Tough economic times, all kinds of people take internships. Besides, we couldn't set you up as another fashion mogul. Hampstead would see through that faster than you go through that damn candy."

"An *intern*?" she repeated and almost choked on the candy. Her throat burned, and she coughed.

"We'll take a few years off you. And get you a younger haircut."

"What's wrong with my hair?" She picked up her smartphone and looked at her reflection in its blank screen.

"Please. You're about to enter the world of competitive dressing. They probably have secret arenas for their clothing wars. You need to look polished—not too polished—and definitely not cop." He set the remote on his desk and picked up his soda again.

"What does 'definitely not cop' mean, exactly?"

Rick grinned again.

"No. Rick, this is not going to work. I'm the last person for this job. What about Sue? She's pretty. Put together. And she reads *Cosmo*. Bet she knows about this fashion stuff."

"Sue's good, but you have much more undercover experience."

"Good time to break her in."

Rick set his soda down and crossed his arms, which made him look like some ancient guardian statue. "You have the experience and the chops for this assignment. Hampstead can be intimidating."

"Sue can be a total hard-ass."

"But we think your sunny disposition makes you the better match for Hampstead's personality."

"That sounds really wrong."

He laughed. "Don't worry. We'll get you ready for it, and we even got you a fashion consultant."

She stared. "I dress fine. No complaints from anybody." She chewed the rest of her candy.

He cocked his head. "Not for this assignment. Didn't you see *The Devil Wears Prada*?"

"That right there is what this is. And Sue is a way better fit. Have you seen her when she's in street clothes?"

"Sorry, Els. You're the pick."

She glared at him. "There's no guarantee I'll get the job, anyway." She reached for another candy.

"Not to worry. Here's the folder on you and your new past." He handed it to her. "You do have to knock 'em dead in the interview. Well, halfway dead will work, because Hampstead's reputation as a bitch on wheels, I believe you said, means they're not going to care too much what warm body occupies an internship. Temporary jobs like that, no problem."

She popped the fresh candy into her mouth. "When's the interview?"

"Three days."

She coughed again.

"You'll need to pack a few things. You'll be based out of an apartment in Brooklyn, close to the bridge. It's fully furnished, so just take clothes and sundries. Maybe some food."

"Oh, yeah. That," Ellie muttered.

Rick grinned. "And right now, you need to meet with your fashion consultant so she can get a sense of you and all your skin tones and your seasonal palette. Or however that works. I'm thinking you're more spring," he said as he motioned toward the door. "Though I know some blondes who look good in fall colors."

"You're enjoying this far too much."

"You have no idea."

She grabbed another candy and followed him, wondering if combat boots were a thing yet at Fashion Forward.

Ellie watched another video from the recent Fashion Week in the city—which had taken place a couple of weeks ago. Marya Hampstead had given a rare, two-minute interview. She was almost cordial in this one, though still a little prickly. Okay, Ellie conceded. She was attractive, and someone who would turn Ellie's head in a crowd. A helpful trait in the fashion industry, too, which relied on that sort of surface appeal. Plus, she sounded good. Articulate, well-formed sentences in a clear British accent. That probably got her major points on the American circuit. Because who didn't love a James Bond-ish British accent on this side of the pond? That had to be hot, whispering in your ear with that.

She clicked to another video. This one showed Hampstead entering a trendy nightclub in Los Angeles over Christmas. She gave a perfunctory wave to the paparazzi—seriously? They stalked fashion moguls, too?—and went in, with a guy on her arm who looked like he could have been a linebacker for the NFL. Ellie had seen the same guy in a few other videos, but Hampstead's file said he was part of her security detail.

Ellie ran the video back and paid more attention to the body language between him and Hampstead. Seemed platonic. But you never knew. Didn't lots of straight female celebrity types bang one of their bodyguards now and then? She grinned. Probably lots of straight-acting celebrity dudes did, too. In this case, given Marya's looks and accent, hell, if Ellie worked security for her, she'd want to hit it with the fashion queen, too.

Her coffee was cold, but she drank it anyway as she ordered Chinese delivery. She'd spent the last two days in her apartment, studying Marya Hampstead, and memorizing her own background that Rick had provided. At least they let her keep her first name. Ellie recited her new life history again, making sure it came naturally. She already had a bunch of her regular clothes ready to go to the new apartment, and supposedly, the department was dropping off some clothing there from the fashion consultant.

Christ. Fashion consultant. Ellie made a face, though the consultant was professional and actually easy to work with. Still, she'd never thought those two words would ever be mentioned in conjunction with her name or an assignment.

The department had also constructed a social media presence for her new self, and her handlers were ensuring that it was updated with relevant info. She wondered how many of the followers were fake as she scrolled through her posts and Tweets about news in the fashion industry, cute dogs, some cooking stuff—her new self was quite the cosmopolitan type. But not too much. Nothing that would draw questions or comments. The goal was to get mostly benign "likes."

Ellie had made a few posts herself, just to get used to it, since she didn't maintain a presence in her real life. Being in law enforcement precluded that, and she preferred a low profile.

Her food arrived, and she moved her laptop to her coffee table so she could eat on her couch while she worked. Hampstead had been into fashion from an early age. Kind of weird, to be all obsessed with fashion like that all those years. Ellie wondered if Hampstead couched everything she talked about in fashion. If someone mentioned the weather, would she bust out the fall line or something?

Ellie's phone rang, and she groaned when Gwen's name showed in the ID. She set her carton down and answered. "Hey. What's up?"

"Hi, Ellie. Sorry to bother you, but do you think I could get my blender this weekend?"

"I'm not sure I'll be around. Can I drop it by your office tomorrow afternoon? I'll just leave it with Trudy." So we don't have to see each other and relive the dissolution of the almost-engagement, she added silently.

"Are you sure?"

"Yeah. It's fine."

"I'll probably be available. We could get coffee." Gwen sounded mostly professional.

"Thanks for the offer, but—"

"I understand," she said, and she sounded sad.

"No, it's not that."

Gwen waited, and Ellie hated that she could still read her.

"Okay," Ellie admitted. "It is kind of that. I'm not ready yet. But I also just started a new assignment, and you know how that goes."

Yeah, Gwen knew only too well how that went. Ellie's weird hours, how she couldn't talk much about her work, how she used her job to avoid intimacy—all the things that made Gwen call it quits.

"Maybe next time." Gwen filled the space easily, saving Ellie from having to talk anymore about the fact that after ten months, she still didn't want to deal with her face-to-face. "I really appreciate that you'll drop the blender off. I think that might be the last of my stuff over there."

"If I find anything else, I'll let you know."

"Thanks. And Ellie, I still care about you. Just because we didn't work as partners doesn't mean we can't work as friends. Talk to you later." She hung up before Ellie could respond, and it was probably just as well, since Ellie didn't have a response anyway.

It had been a bad idea, getting involved with a lawyer. How could that even have worked? Especially since Gwen was more the settling down type and Ellie really wasn't. For now. Gwen had figured it out and let her down easy, everything considered, though Ellie had to cancel the order on the engagement ring. The whole breakup could've gone a lot worse. And eventually, she'd have coffee and maybe even a meal with Gwen. Just not right now. She picked up her food and clicked onto another link about Marya Hampstead, and as she chewed, she decided she should find another law enforcement type if she wanted a relationship.

CHAPTER 2

"Damn."

"Don't even." Ellie glared at Rick, and he laughed.

"Maybe we'll keep the fashion consultant on a bit longer."

She flipped him off. "I'm not even going to dignify the inherent sexism of that with a comment."

"You just did." He grinned.

She flipped him off with both hands and strode purposefully across the room to her desk, pleased that she could do it in heels and look badass, too. The other guys in the room went silent.

"What?" she snapped at the closest two.

"Nothing," they both said as they looked away.

"Who knew O'Donnell was a woman?" another guy said from the other side of the room, bringing a bunch of snorts and laughs.

"So all it takes is a skirt and a pair of heels?" someone else joined in. "Let's get the consultant to work on you," she said to the other guy.

"Nah, it's the haircut." Rick flashed Ellie a grin.

"Shit, O'Donnell. You're about as hot as Hampstead is."

"Shut up, Wes." Ellie hadn't had her hair this short since her recruit days. She put a handful of cinnamon Jolly Ranchers into the handbag she'd been given to coordinate with the outfit she wore. "And be glad I don't have my boots on." She gave him a look and did a drag queen snap.

Several of the guys whooped and laughed. Ellie grabbed another handful of candy. This was probably going to be at least a ten-piece day. She put the short jacket on that matched her skirt, black suede with smooth black leather accents. The consultant had recommended something with classic lines but a little edgier. Hence the black suede/black leather and the light gray shirt that sported burgundy collar tips. She'd provided a pair of black suede heels and neutral hose to complete the outfit.

Ellie picked up her handbag as well as the large canvas tote bag that held Gwen's blender. Rick frowned when he saw it.

"What?" Ellie hefted it. "We're in New York. People carry all kinds of shit all the time with them. Besides," she added, "it gives me a little extra credence. I'm a busy woman, dammit, and I have places to be after this interview."

He shrugged. "A blender? I'd have gone for another pair of shoes."

"They're in there, too." She addressed the rest of the staff in the room. "Here's your show." She flashed her most charming smile and sashayed toward the door, drawing cheers and whistles.

"Work it, O'Donnell," Rick said behind her. "I knew you'd be perfect for this job."

"It's only because I look better in heels than you do."

"That's totally it. Better than any of the guys here."

"Don't knock it." She used her hip to push the door open to the parking lot. Rick gestured at one of the unmarked cars that didn't look as much like a cop car as the others.

"To reiterate," he said as he pulled into traffic, which would only get worse once they hit midtown Manhattan, "We've got a team across the street and two floors above Fashion Forward, if you need anything or something goes nuts."

"Rundell Realty," Ellie recited. "And across the street, thirty-third floor, Wi-Tech."

"What's your name?"

"Ellie Daniels."

"Where are you from?" Rick glanced at her, as traffic crawled.

"Indianapolis."

"Date of birth?"

"July twentieth, 1987."

"We took four years and change off you. How does it feel?"

Ellie took a cinnamon candy out of her purse. "My knee still bugs me a little. Can we go back a few more years?"

"We aren't miracle workers," he deadpanned. "Where'd you go to school?"

"Indiana University. I majored in business but did theater on the side and got really into costume design. Love me some community theater," she deadpanned back at him.

"Where were you before you decided to chase your high-fashion dreams?"

"Wayne and Stevens, doing ad copy."

"So what kind of toilet paper does Hampstead use?"

"She's a Charmin girl, all the way."

Rick looked at her, since they were at a red light. "Seriously?"

"Nah. I figured that when the help wipes her ass, they'd want to use a soft brand."

He chuckled. "Too much. How do you feel?"

"Same as I ever do before a new assignment."

"You'll rock this role, too. What's your current address?"

She recited it back to him, the apartment just over the river in Brooklyn.

"Good." He stopped the car a couple of blocks from the Fashion Forward building without trying to find a spot along the curb, drawing several honks from people trying to get around him. He held his fist out and Ellie bumped it with hers.

"Kick it," he said, his standard well-wish.

She grabbed her purse and tote bag. "Thanks, sweetie," she said, and she leaned in and pecked him on the cheek. "In case anybody's watching."

"I may never wash this cheek."

"Dude. Chicks don't dig dirty cheeks." She was out of the car before he could snap another retort.

Since she hadn't worn heels in a while, Ellie kept her pace even and stayed near the buildings. It would not rock if she face-planted in the streams of pedestrians on the sidewalk. Plus, heels clearly made things like blenders heavier. She'd be glad to dump it off at Gwen's after this. She made it to Fashion Forward without any embarrassing incidents and checked in with the security guards at the counter in the lobby—one of those marble-and-glass affairs designed to look corporate and impressive. They provided a temporary passcard that allowed access to the elevator. Once on board, she hit the button for the thirty-first floor.

After a quiet ride up, the doors opened into a carpeted, tasteful foyer, and Ellie pushed through the glass doors into the lobby for Fashion Forward, which was nearly as impressive as the first floor's, and far more stylish. The colors here popped, as the appropriate terminology went, but not in an annoying or distracting way. Lots of blues and greens with splashes of red on the upholstery of the chairs and area rugs. Art that was probably done by important people hung on the walls, lending even more color and vibrancy to what otherwise would probably have been a sterile corporate space. Hampstead and her people clearly knew how to do decorating, too.

"Hello," Ellie said to the receptionist, dropping her voice a little to sound a bit more sultry. "I have an eleven o'clock with Tyler Jackson."

"Ah, yes. He'll be right out, Ms. Daniels." The receptionist smiled at her, all sleek business, but clearly ready for the runway herself, since she had the lithe look of a model. "Would you like some coffee?"

"I would love some."

"Do you have a preference?"

"Regular, a splash of cream."

Beautiful Receptionist got up and went through the open door behind her. Ellie set the bag with the blender on the floor, thinking that Gwen did totally owe her a cup of coffee, at least, because the damn thing was heavy and lugging it around New York hadn't been one of Ellie's better ideas.

Fashion Forward had a lot of traffic, with people coming and going through the lobby. No Russian arms dealers, she was pretty sure. Yet.

"Here you are," Beautiful Receptionist said, and Ellie took the cup from her.

"Thank you so much." She sniffed then tasted a bit. Of course there would be beautiful coffee here, too. That was a definite perk to this assignment.

"Hi, Ms. Daniels? I'm Tyler." Another beautiful person. Tyler Jackson was a generically handsome, slim white man with impeccably styled hair, exquisitely trimmed goatee, and a button-down, blue pinstripe shirt that probably cost a couple hundred dollars tucked into equally expensive gray trousers. His tasteful bowtie added to his fashion mag looks.

"Oh, good," he said. "You've already got coffee." He gestured at her cup and smiled at the receptionist. "My office is right over here." He smiled at Ellie, too, and she made sure her purse strap was stable on her shoulder before she picked up the tote bag.

They went through a set of glass double doors into a hallway beyond, also tastefully appointed in great colors and excellent art. Tyler's office was down the hall to the left, and he had a great view of the city. He sat down behind his desk—an urban Ikea-looking thing—with his back to the view. All the furnishings in his office looked as if they'd come out of a Swedish furniture showroom.

"Please, sit," he said. "How are you on that coffee?"

"Fine, thanks." She took one of the chairs that faced his desk, grateful to put the blender down. He had a copy of her résumé on his desk.

"So, Eleanor—can I call you Eleanor?" He looked at her over his desk.

"It's Ellie. And yes, you can call me Ellie." She smiled. Gwen had said Ellie's smile could charm practically anyone. Tyler nodded, seeming to be happy about that. He was pinging Ellie's gaydar, though she generally thought of big cowboys on the covers of heterosexual romance novels when men were named Tyler. She'd have to finish her dossier on him in the next couple of days.

"Excellent. So, Ellie, why are you interested in an internship at Fashion Forward?"

She crossed her legs—carefully, since she was wearing a skirt—and gestured at her completely fabricated résumé. "As you already know, I was involved in theater during college as a costume designer. I've been doing that on the side since, but I also volunteer at fashion venues. After the most recent Fashion Week, I decided I wanted to get more involved in the industry. An internship here, I think, will provide invaluable experience and hopefully some ideas for what aspect I'd like to pursue in greater depth." That sounded pretty good, she thought. Not too stupid.

He nodded and sat back in his chair. He propped his elbows on the armrests and steepled his fingers. "I understand that. But the question is, why Fashion Forward?"

"Marya Hampstead is known internationally, and her work at this company has set numerous trends. When people want to know what's next, they look here."

"As good as that sounds, I'm assuming that you've also heard the rumors." A trace of a smile graced his perfect lips.

Ellie leaned back, making herself look more relaxed and confident. "I'm guessing you're implying the rumors about Ms. Hampstead's reputation with staff."

"And everyone else, yes." He studied her, and it was a little unnerving, like a spider scoping out a bug.

She studied him back. "It's irrelevant. This internship isn't permanent, and I want to learn whatever I can from Ms. Hampstead and the staff at Fashion Forward."

He smiled again, and it seemed genuine. "Excellent. When can you start?"

That knocked her back a little, but she recovered quickly. "Monday." It was already Friday, so why not? Wasn't like she was getting out of this assignment. She might as well get it over with.

"Super. If you have some time now, I can show you around and get you set up with our human resources department."

Her expression must have broadcast her confusion because he laughed, and that, too, was genuine. "Look, the reality is, if anyone is willing to be an intern here with Ms. Hampstead, then we go with it." He stood, and she did, too.

"So the rumors are true?" she asked, looking to forge a little bit of a bond with him and remembering what Rick had said about Hampstead's reputation and how practically any warm body would do.

"Oh, yes," he said, eyes seeming to twinkle.

"You're not even going to take me in for an interview with her?"

"Oh, no. I'm her long-suffering senior staffer. She relies on me to do the hiring and firing, and I generally have a good idea about who's going to work out—meaning, who's going to be able to complete the internship—and who's not. Ready?" He came around the desk and gestured toward the door.

As Tyler walked her around the various offices on the floor, Ellie studied the layout, listening, nodding, and smiling appropriately as he chatted about who did what in terms of the magazines Fashion Forward handled. She'd get a better sense come Monday, but for now, she watched how others responded to Tyler. Since he was Hampstead's senior staffer, they might think he was her spy. For the most part, however, she didn't get that sense from the other employees. Maybe they all banded together as protection from the dragon lady.

"Here are all the forms we need you to fill out," Tyler said after he'd taken her to the HR office. "Bring them back with you on Monday. We'll get a copy of your driver's license then."

"Thank you." She took the papers and slid them into the tote bag. "And thank you so much for this wonderful opportunity."

"Let me know in a couple of weeks if you still feel that way." He smiled, and his cell phone rang with Madonna's "Vogue." Ellie barely managed not to laugh.

"We'll see you Monday at nine," he said as he took his phone out of his pocket. "Can you find your way out?"

"Yes."

"Excellent." He answered the call, and Ellie left.

She walked slowly toward the main lobby, hating the blender but hoping she might get a look at the legendary Queen Bitch of Fashion Forward, but alas, such was not to be. Staffers moved purposefully around her, and the beautiful receptionist nodded at her as she left. At least three men checked her out before she got to the elevator, and she decided that the woman Rick had lined up to do Straight Eye for the Lesbian on her must've done her job right. She hardly ever wore skirts or heels, but she knew how to rock both if she had to.

Except right now, she really wanted to adjust the crotch of her hose. And she really needed to be a little more careful with walking because she tripped as she got off the elevator. Smooth. She caught herself and blamed it on the blender. Once outside, she set the bag with the blender down and dug in her purse and put her sunglasses on. The air was a little humid and warm for late September, though she knew it might change in the next couple of days. Weather in this city was always dicey.

She somehow managed to hail a cab, which pulled over almost immediately—a miracle. As she moved toward it, a man who looked familiar walked past her. Daddy Hampstead. Interesting. She waited for a moment, assessing, and decided to follow Marya Hampstead's father for a while. So she waved the cab away, regretting it because it was the fastest she'd ever gotten one, and walked after Jonathan Hampstead, her persona just another New Yorker carrying a bunch of crap.

He didn't go into the Fashion Forward building, though he gave it a glance as he passed. And then a couple more. Ellie knew that trick. He was checking reflections in the glass. She stopped and pretended to dig around in her purse, also checking the reflections.

Well. That was also interesting. A couple of guys dressed in very sharp suits caught her eye. They were crossing the street behind her, coming toward the Fashion Forward building. And they stuck out because they weren't talking to each other. Instead, their gazes were locked onto Daddy Hampstead. They looked like a Russian security detail. Or something much worse. The shorter of the two reached inside his suit jacket in a way that indicated he probably had a gun.

She stopped rummaging in her purse and walked briskly after Marya's father, which wasn't a big deal in New York. Everybody who wasn't a tourist walked fast here. Including the heavies behind her. Jonathan Hampstead stopped as if he was studying something in the window of a clothing store. The heavies stopped, too. Ellie slowed her pace, and pretended to dig in the tote bag with the blender for something. She was like a damn archaeologist, sifting through all her crap all the time. Jonathan moved to the door of the shop, looking like any other casual shopper, like he had all the time in the world.

He went inside, and the Russians bolted toward the store. Ellie acted, deciding that it wouldn't do this op any good if Daddy Hampstead was either killed or kidnapped—

or both—by Russian gangsters. So she tripped and fell toward one of the men, swinging the tote bag as if she was trying to keep her balance. She ran into the one guy, and the blender-laden bag connected with the knee of the other. Hard. He yelped and staggered back while the other guy tried to disentangle himself from her.

"Oh, my God. I am so sorry," she said as she pushed off the man she'd run into, catching a whiff of his cologne. Something sweet, like 1980s Polo. "Are you okay?"

"Yes, I am all right," he muttered in accented English.

"I'm so sorry," she said to the taller guy, who was limping a little, trying to walk it off. He said something in Russian, face dark with anger. A few other people slowed, curious at what had happened, then continued on their way when it was clear it was nothing serious or interesting enough for them to film and post on social media.

"Can I get you an ice pack?" she continued, looking around as if there was an ice pack stand somewhere. "I'm so, so sorry. I can be so clumsy. My friends are always telling me that. Are you sure you don't need an ice pack? I have some Advil—"

"No," the taller man snapped. He said something to his companion in Russian, and they hurried to the store Hampstead had gone into.

"Are you sure you're okay?" Ellie called after them, but they ignored her. She checked the blender. Good thing Gwen had bought a seriously solid one. The thick glass was fine, and the motor part looked okay, too. She'd provided Hampstead a little extra time to go out the back. For a businessman, he seemed pretty savvy about potential street fights. Maybe he watched a lot of thriller movies.

She flagged down another cab, and this one took its New York time, but once she settled in its interior, she checked the area outside the store Hampstead had gone into. The Russians hadn't come out of it, yet. They'd probably gone out the back, too. She sucked on another candy, knowing that her weekend work now included slogging through tons of photos of local Russian gangsters. Halfway to Gwen's office, Ellie texted her: "Let me know if anything's weird with the blender. I'll buy you a new one."

CHAPTER 3

"Those things'll kill you," Rick said. He set a fresh cup of coffee on her desk as he picked up the pile of candy wrappers with his other hand and threw them in her nearby trash can.

"Oh, and this won't?" Ellie gestured at the coffee.

"At least it's not full of sugar and red dye number ninety-two or whatever. So, have you figured out who was messing with Daddy Hampstead?" He perched on the edge of her desk, and even though it was Saturday, he wore dark trousers and a button-down shirt open at the collar. She knew he kept a couple of ties neatly folded in one of his desk drawers, in case he needed to "represent," as he called it. She, however, wore jeans and an NYPD polo shirt.

"Pretty sure this is the shorter guy." She adjusted her monitor so he could better see.

"He looks familiar."

"Leo Zaretsky ring any bells?" she asked as she printed his photo and the little bit of information on him.

Rick didn't answer for a bit as he sipped his coffee. For such a big, muscular dude, he took his coffee seriously and sipped delicately. "Oh, yeah. Got it," he finally said. "He runs with the Petrovs."

"Priors on this guy?"

"Never been able to nail him for anything. Dude's slick, like most of them are."

Ellie sipped her own coffee and stared at the screen. "So chances are the other guy hangs with the Petrovs, too."

"That'd be my guess."

"Mr. Unknown is the guy with a sore knee today after he ran into the blender in my bag." She unwrapped another cinnamon candy, and Rick frowned. She popped it into her mouth. "What?" she said at Rick's expression. "You should try one. Gives a whole new dimension to coffee."

Rick pushed off her desk. "Guess it was a good thing you had that blender with you. Speaking of which, why did you? Trying new techniques for undercover weaponry?"

She snorted. "If only. It's Gwen's. I took it back to her yesterday."

His expression remained impassive. "And how's that going?"

"You mean how are things with my former almost-fiancée, who I still can't be around for more than a few minutes after ten months?"

He sipped his coffee and watched her.

"We're civil. She's much nicer than I am. But then, that's not hard to do. I'm not the easiest person to live with."

"Who is?" He gave her a shrug. "So, anybody interesting on the dating horizon?"

"Why no, Dr. Phil. And would you also like to know what toilet paper I use?"

He grinned. "Already do. So how about we grab a beer later?"

"Sure. What time?"

He glanced at his watch. She liked that about him, that he wore one. Not something you saw much anymore. "It's almost three-thirty now. Six?"

"Sounds good. See you there." She didn't have to ask where. They always went to the same out-of-the-way neighborhood bar that catered to cops and jocks, the two not always mutually exclusive.

"Later." He picked up his blazer from his desk chair and left. She turned back to the screen and continued her quest to ID Mr. Unknown, aka Mr. Sore Knee. Ninety minutes later, she still hadn't found anything on him in US law enforcement databases so she tried Interpol. Ten minutes later, she found him. Mr. Sore Knee had a name and a record.

"Well, hello, Mr. Yuri Laskin," Ellie muttered as she printed out his photo and the summary of his bad deeds, which included fraud, arms dealing, and several assaults. He was also wanted for questioning in a couple of high-profile murders in Berlin. Last known sighting was in Warsaw three months ago. Until yesterday. *International criminal sidelined by blender injury.* Ellie sat back. The Petrovs seemed to be targeting Jonathan Hampstead. Why?

She'd try to find out. But not until tomorrow. Ellie shut down her computer, gathered her things, and left, knowing that there were two things she could count on at the moment. Rick would beat her to the bar, and he'd have her beer waiting.

Second day at the new job, and Ellie arrived at Fashion Forward early. For all the things the guys teased her about, tardiness was not one of them. She yawned. She'd settled into the new apartment Sunday night, and she'd had a hard time sleeping as she adjusted to the sounds of the new location.

The elevator dinged, and she stepped in with a few other people. She ended up next to the buttons and was about to press hers when four other people crowded on, in a cloud of varying degrees of cologne. This was clearly Ellie's lucky day, because one of them was Marya Hampstead.

"Floor?" Ellie asked her as if she didn't know. Three impeccably dressed young men served as Hampstead's entourage, and they glanced nervously at each other and at Hampstead, who was on her cell phone, ignoring them in that way that people who wielded power had.

"Thirty-one. Thank you," she said to Ellie before returning to her phone convo. She hadn't taken her gajillion-dollar sunglasses off.

Ellie didn't have to press the number because she already had done it for herself. She leaned back against the elevator's wall, pretending to check her phone. Okay, Marya Hampstead was seriously attractive in person, even without all the fashion spread airbrushing. Today, she had kind of a classy glamour thing going on, with a slim black skirt suit with white accents and tasteful—oh, my God, did she just use that word in her inventory about another person?—black heels. Hampstead's dark hair was piled onto her head in a way that made it look carefree, but Ellie was sure she probably had someone work on it for an hour. Lucky stylist, getting to run their fingers through Hampstead's hair.

"That's *your* problem, isn't it? If you can't provide a quality product by the expected deadline, I'll find someone who can," Hampstead said in her smooth British accent to the unfortunate party on the other end of the phone. Everything sounded good with that accent, including a tongue-lashing. Which conjured other, far more vivid and inappropriate images for Ellie as she surreptitiously admired the way Hampstead filled her clothes. Not a good idea, to have the hots for the target. She studied her phone again to keep herself from checking her out more.

The elevator stopped at fifteen, leaving Ellie with Hampstead and her entourage and one other man.

"No product, no payment, no further business," Hampstead said, and though she hadn't raised her voice, the temperature in the elevator seemed to drop. The three men looked at each other again, still nervous.

"I expect so," Hampstead said with finality and hung up.

Ouch to whoever that was. Ellie moved a little so the non-Hampstead guy could exit at the twentieth floor, and that put Hampstead within inches of her. Ellie inhaled a little, curious about Hampstead's cologne. Whatever it was, it was understated with just a trace of something citrusy. She approved. Some people drenched themselves in cologne, like Leo Zaretsky last week.

"I want to see the latest layouts before lunch," Hampstead said to the three pretty boys. Her tone left no room for argument. Or even chatting. They all nodded in unison at her, but remained silent. Probably for the best. The elevator stopped and the doors slid open. Marya Hampstead got off first and her entourage followed. Everybody stopped what they were doing and greeted her as she passed. She tossed them all dismissive waves, and the three guys with her peeled off and went to do whatever it was they were supposed to do with the layouts.

Ellie could see how Hampstead got her rep, but on the other hand, she appreciated a woman who wouldn't be pushed around. Nobody paid attention to Ellie as she walked through the lobby, but that was fine. The less noticeable she was, the more information she could gather and, hopefully, the sooner she'd be done with this assignment.

"Hi," Ellie said to her officemate when she entered.

Liz, a perky brunette who looked like she should probably be posing for photos in a Midwestern cornfield, glanced up from what looked like some printouts of a magazine spread. "Oh, hi. I put a page on your desk to check. Just proofreading on some ad copy. Nothing too scary, since it's only your second day."

"Okay." Ellie set her bag on the floor under her desk and took her blazer off, which she hung on the sleek coat rack near the door. "Want some coffee?"

"Love some. Italian roast."

"Okay. Be right back." Ellie smoothed the front of her skirt and went back to the main reception area. Beautiful Receptionist smiled at her as she passed the circular counter and went through the doorway into a kitchenette where the coffee machine was, with a variety of high-end flavors and strengths. She loaded up a pod for Liz and waited for the cup to fill. A guy came in, and Ellie recognized him from the elevator ride up as one of Marya's morning posse. Dark hair, perfectly styled, medium height, slender, bowtie. Dapper.

She smiled at him in greeting, and he gave her a blank stare before he checked the display rack of available coffee pods and removed one from the French roast slot. He tapped it nervously on the counter as he checked his phone. Ellie stepped aside so he could load his pod up. If he was still in Marya's crosshairs, he probably was in a bigger hurry than she was.

Once the machine had filled his cup, he took it and headed for the doorway just as somebody else entered. Ellie saw what was coming, and she winced as the newcomer bumped into Mr. Dapper. The coffee splashed onto his shirt, and he jumped back, swearing, trying to hold what was left in the cup out from his body.

"Shit," said the new arrival, a man Ellie didn't recognize. "I'm so sorry."

Mr. Dapper set the half-empty cup on the counter and pulled several paper towels out of the dispenser. "Fuck," he said woefully as he dabbed at the big brown splotch on his chest. Too bad his shirt was light blue.

"Are you okay? Did you get burned?" the new arrival asked.

"No," he said. "At least not yet. The coffee was for Ms. H."

Ellie imagined him putting his hand to his head in an "oh, no" motion.

"Oh, shit," the other guy said.

Ellie watched the exchange with interest. Ms. H was probably Hampstead, she guessed. "Do you have another shirt?"

He looked at her. "Yes, but Ms. H needs her coffee in—" he looked at his phone. "Seven minutes. I can't go into her office looking like this."

Hampstead had clearly earned her dragon lady rep. "Go change your shirt," Ellie said. "I'll take her coffee in." She loaded up another French roast pod, slid a cup under the spout, and hit start.

"She takes it—"

"Black. I noticed." Ellie smiled at him. "I'm Ellie, for future reference."

"Khalil."

She looked at the other guy, also dapper, but blond and a lot taller. "Marco," he said.

"Nice to meet you." She removed the cup from the machine. "I take it she doesn't do lids."

"Hates them," Khalil said.

Of course she did. "Okay, then. If you would drop this cup—" she handed Liz's covered coffee to Marco—"To Liz over in the office a few doors down from Tyler Jackson, I'd be much obliged. That gives Khalil here a chance to go to his office and change."

Marco handed him the purple folder he was holding. "Cover up," he said, and Khalil took it and held it over the stain on his shirt.

"Thank you," he said to them both. "Three minutes." He ducked out.

"Seriously?" Ellie muttered. Marco apparently heard her, because he stared at her, wide-eyed.

"Have you not met her?" he asked in a hushed tone.

"This'll be the first time." She picked up the coffee cup.

"Oh, my God. You're new."

"Brand spankin'. Wish me luck. And get that coffee to Liz."

He nodded and followed her back into the reception area. Ellie walked purposefully toward the dragon lady's office, which was, of course, in a corner location, so it probably had amazing views all around. And whatever else rich and powerful people kept in corner offices. Maybe hot tubs and full bars. Dance floors? Nice furniture, at the very least.

She held the coffee carefully as she approached the double doors, preparing for either a body to come flying out after tangling with Hampstead or Hampstead herself yanking the doors open imperiously to gaze upon her minions.

Neither happened. In fact, one of the doors was partially open. They swung inward, so Ellie stepped forward and knocked twice on the open door. Hampstead probably didn't like people entering her office without permission, even if the door was open.

"Yes," came the response. It was kind of hot, that one word in Hampstead's accent. She'd like to hear Marya say it again, under very different circumstances.

"Your coffee," Ellie said as she entered, fighting an urge to add "m'lady."

Hampstead was standing at a nearby conference table, sleek and urban chic, like the rest of her tasteful and

Euro-minimalist office. The table was covered with layouts for one of Fashion Forward's publications.

Hampstead surprised Ellie by taking the coffee from her directly rather than ordering her to put it somewhere. And Ellie had been right. She was surrounded by views of the city out the two walls of windows. But the view of Hampstead was much better.

"Thank you," Hampstead said, adding another layer of surprise with the politeness. "And you are?"

"Ellie Daniels. Intern. Pleasure to meet you, Ms. Hampstead." She didn't offer her hand because Hampstead's body language didn't suggest a handshake.

"You were on the elevator this morning." She seemed to be studying Ellie, sizing her up. And clearly, the sunglasses Hampstead had worn that morning were designed to keep people from getting caught in her eyes, because that's exactly what happened to Ellie.

"I was," Ellie said, pleased she didn't sound like she was admiring the shifting shades of gray in the eyes of the dragon lady.

Hampstead sipped the coffee. "Tyler did mention that he'd hired someone. And where is Khalil?" Her tone wasn't demanding. Rather, the question was just something she tacked onto the end of the sentence, like, "did you remember your umbrella?"

"A phone call in the coffee room." Ellie met Hampstead's abrupt change of topic just as smoothly as Hampstead had injected it. "Something about the layouts. He said he absolutely had to attend to it in order to ensure you got the correct draft or something to that effect. He threw himself on my mercy to bring you coffee. He'll be here in a few minutes."

"I see." If Hampstead was skeptical, it didn't show on her face. Fortunately, a knock at her door interrupted whatever Hampstead was going to say next. Marco poked his head in, tentative, as if he was dreading having to clean up a scorch mark in the carpet that had been Ellie Daniels, intrepid intern. He seemed shocked to see her standing a few feet from Hampstead, unscathed.

"Ms. H?" he said to Hampstead. "Are you ready for the meeting?"

She nodded, brusque, and motioned at the table. He came in, followed by a few other young men, a couple of men who looked to be in their forties, and three women, two in their thirties, Ellie gauged.

"Nice to finally meet you," Ellie said to Hampstead as she left, not expecting a response. She ducked out of the office and saw Khalil hurrying toward her in the corridor, wearing a different shirt. "Here's your cover story. You took a phone call in the coffee room about the layouts," Ellie said to him with a grin. "And enlisted my help delivering the coffee."

"Thank you," he said as he rushed past. "Are you okay?"

"Fine."

He hesitated, as if he wanted to ask her another question, but went into the office instead. Ellie went back to the coffee room to get herself a cup before she went back to her own office.

Hampstead hadn't been quite what she'd expected. Maybe Ellie had caught her on a good day, even with the incident on the elevator. And interesting, how Hampstead had remembered her. She paid attention, and that could be a problem since Ellie had wanted to stay under Hampstead's radar. She figured Hampstead would just dismiss her as one of the many acolytes roaming the halls of Fashion Forward, but it didn't look like that was going to happen.

Hampstead was also much more attractive in person than in photos and videos, and it didn't have much to do with her physical appearance, which was nice, but rather with her eyes. Ellie had caught a glimpse of their depths beneath the armor of the dragon lady, and in spite of herself and this assignment, she wanted another look.

Coffee in hand, she checked her hair in the reflection afforded by the microwave door and went back to her office.

CHAPTER 4

"Anything?" Ellie leaned back in her chair and stared at the ceiling as she held her phone to her ear.

"She's still at dinner," Rick said. "Same people she went in with."

Ellie had already identified them. Khalil, Tyler, a guy Hampstead used for security, and the other one was a designer with his own two-man posse. "It's been a week since I messed up Laskin's knee," she said. "Anything new on Daddy Hampstead?"

"Nothing that you didn't track down."

She frowned. "Media says he's still in Los Angeles. Our buddies out there confirm he's attending a business summit, and there's no sign of his Russian friends."

"So maybe he just pissed somebody off in New York."

"Him and seven million other people in this city," Ellie said. "Could be they figure it's easier to fuck him up when he's here, since he's been here four times already in the past five months. All they have to do is wait for him to show up."

Rick grunted. "Something smells. Why would a guy like Laskin be hanging out with the Petrovs?"

"And why would they target Hampstead?" Ellie stared harder at the ceiling, as if it would suddenly open and reveal all the secrets of this case.

"If Koslov is running guns, maybe Hampstead is the money guy."

Ellie pondered that. "Not a bad idea." She sat up, her feet hitting the floor with a plop. "What if Hampstead is the dude who ordered the hits on the Petrovs?"

Rick didn't say anything for a few moments. "He's going behind Daddy Koslov's back? Getting rid of the competition?"

"Why not? He doesn't have to ask anything. He just tells Hampstead to take care of it, and then he has deniability. So the Petrovs maybe found out and hired a couple of guys to take care of Hampstead."

"All right," Rick said. "I could buy that. But we don't have the evidence that Hampstead is in on this. So the next line of business is, let's see if we can tie Hampstead to our three dead men. And did you try to find any family connections between Laskin and the Petrovs?"

"Yeah. Nothing yet."

"Might not be by blood. He could've married into the family."

"Good point, but Laskin's Interpol info doesn't list a wife. And maybe he's been hired for business only, on recommendation."

"True, but these guys tend to keep shit like that hidden. Maybe he's divorced, or maybe he's in deep with the Petrovs and owes them a favor or two."

Ellie idly clicked one of her browser tabs and Marya Hampstead filled her laptop screen. Another celebrity sighting article from last week. She wore her sunglasses in this image, but her hair fell in dark waves around her shoulders, and the collar of her blouse was open just enough to make a person look a little farther down without sacrificing modesty. Ellie closed the window. Not good, getting caught up like that.

"Do you think they'll try to use Marya to get to Jonathan?"

"The thought did cross my mind," Rick said, "but I think her celebrity status probably protects her. The last thing the Petrovs want is a dead or missing internationally known fashion mogul that can be linked to them."

"True." Ellie breathed a little sigh of relief. Sure, Marya might be an arms dealer, but the thought of her getting roughed up by a bunch of Russian mobster assholes—maybe killed—was not something she wanted to contemplate.

"Target's on the move," Rick said. "Out."

He hung up, and she took a swallow of coffee then did another search on her laptop. She had turned down a Friday night out with friends to go to the office and do some more research on Fashion Forward, but she didn't mind as much as she should have. Maybe it was because every photo she came across of Marya Hampstead provided serious eye candy, especially if she wasn't wearing her sunglasses.

Speaking of candy, she unwrapped another one and popped it into her mouth and chased it with another swig of coffee. Rick didn't know what he was missing; lukewarm coffee with a cinnamon blast. She paused at another photo of Hampstead. In this one, a press shot, she wore her trademark enigmatic Mona Lisa smile. Not quite full-blown and just enough mystery to make a person want to know more. She stared at it for a while, then went back through all the information she had on Daddy Hampstead. Nothing jumped out at her. No criminal record. Solid reputation in international banking. The kind of guy you wanted handling your money.

So what the hell did two Russian gangsters want with him? She looked at the photo of Marya Hampstead. Her expression made Ellie think she knew but wasn't about to tell. Okay, fine, Mr. International Man of Mystery. Where had he been over the past year? She ran various searches and constructed a list of business meetings and expos. She typed it up, printed it out, and then checked it against the dates and places that the three dead guys had been found.

And hello, this was interesting. Hampstead had been in Moscow at a banking summit in January two days after the first Petrov turned up dead. And then in March, Hampstead just happened to be in Prague launching a branch office the same day the second Petrov died. Where was Mr. Mystery in June? Oh, look at that. She stared at the list she'd just made and at the date of death for the third murdered man. Hampstead was in London about that time. But then, he was based in London. Except he was in Madrid two days before the London guy turned up dead and then all of a sudden Hampstead was back in London with a day to spare before that guy was killed.

She went back through all the info she had on the Russians. Her money was on Laskin being hired by the Petrovs because maybe, just maybe, Hampstead was ordering hits on their arms dealers overseas. So Marya was running around with Lyev Koslov because her dad was doing all kinds of shit with them. The question was, did she know about it?

Ellie ran several searches but nothing came up except a photo from some high-priced fundraiser four months ago that she'd already seen. Marya was getting out of a limo as Lyev Koslov extended his hand to help her. He was wearing a tux, the perfect male escort. He looked like the male lead in an action film. Ellie scanned the people near the limo, but didn't see either Laskin or Zaretsky. Her research demonstrated that Lyev was more a playboy type and didn't spend a whole lot of time with the family business. Daddy Koslov farmed it out to the older brothers.

"Shit," she muttered as she took another drink of her coffee, now cold. Nothing to tie Laskin to Daddy Hampstead beyond what Ellie had seen on the street and the possibility—unproven—that Hampstead was ordering hits on Petrovs. Fuck this, she decided. How about business-related info? Twenty minutes later, she stumbled across an online article from a UK news source that mentioned a gathering of business heavy-hitters in London a year ago. Daddy Hampstead was mentioned and hello—so was Daddy Koslov.

Okay, so she could tie Koslov to Daddy Hampstead and Koslov's son Lyev to Marya. Was either Hampstead aware of Daddy Koslov's extracurricular activities? It could be a total coincidence that Jonathan Hampstead was in those cities at the times when three different Petrovs died. But she doubted it, because a couple of Russians with Petrov ties were clearly interested in Jonathan Hampstead. Ellie had also run a ton of searches looking for ties between Hampstead and the Petrov family, but had come up blank.

"This is a clusterfuck." She went back through her notes about other staff at Fashion Forward. Tyler Jackson checked out. Originally from Chicago, a nice Midwestern upbringing in the 'burbs, did theater and fashion throughout high school, went to an arts academy and got some local fame for a few of his styles. Ellie had dug around on the connections between Tyler and Marya, and every version of the story was the same. Tyler had been working a spring Fashion Week three years ago and caught Marya's eye. For whatever reasons, people said, she liked him. But Ellie found nothing in his past to suggest nefarious contacts or activities. And the same went with the rest of the staff, though she was having profiles run on all of them just to be sure.

She stood and stretched. Shit like this could get really tangled, and if she pulled on one thread, it just knotted up with a bunch of others. Her phone rang.

"Yeah," she answered.

"She went back to her apartment building," Rick said.

"Who went with her?"

"Rent-a-cop, but he didn't stay. At least, not with her. He's got his team on surveillance, like usual."

That was the big dude Ellie had seen in other pictures. He wouldn't need to stay in Hampstead's apartment, since her building was security-conscious. She wasn't the only celebrity who lived in it. Ellie checked the time. Eleven-thirty. She'd been at the office doing research since she left Fashion Forward at two that afternoon.

"Did you come up with anything else?" he asked.

She filled him in on what she'd found, and when she finished, he whistled through his teeth.

"Now *that's* why I brought you on to this team. I'm going to check in with some of my contacts in the UK who have been looking into this, see if anything comes up with them. Good work."

"So what's going on over there now?"

"Nothing much," Rick said. "We've got the front and back covered. Lights are on in her place. Speaking of, go to the apartment and get some sleep. And eat something healthy. I'll let you know if anything freaky happens."

"Define freaky."

"Els," he said, stern. "You've been on this all day."

She sighed.

"Go. Sleep."

"Thanks, Dad," she said with a grumble before adding, "Bye," in a sing-song voice before she hung up. He was right, though. Her eyes burned, and fatigue had stiffened her back. By the time she got back to the apartment, she was too tired to make a sandwich, so she went straight to bed, and the last thing on her mind was, disconcertingly, Marya Hampstead.

Ellie checked her appearance in the bathroom mirror. Not bad. The fashion consultant had continued with the classic but edgy look, so today's black skirt was slim and professional, but her hose were black accented with tiny black hearts in the pattern. Not something Ellie O'Donnell would wear, but Ellie Daniels would. Plus, you had to look hard to see the hearts, and nobody was getting close enough to her to do that, though she'd totally let Marya Hampstead in for a look.

Ellie grinned at herself in the mirror and smoothed her blouse—gray silk with a slight masculine cut—and checked her earrings, plain silver hoops that matched the buttons of her blouse. Today's shoes were a forties-style heel, classic black, but the retro lines added to the edgy look. Agent Carter-ish, maybe. She nodded at herself.

Done in the bathroom, she returned to her office for some files. Liz looked up at her from her own desk.

"How do I look?" Ellie asked, though she already knew she looked fine.

"Very nice. Too bad you didn't consider being a model."

"I don't look like a stick figure. Besides, I like food."

Liz giggled, then frowned. "Are you ready for the meeting?"

"As ready as I'll ever be."

"Good luck."

Ellie gave her a thumbs-up and left for her first official layouts meeting with Marya Hampstead and the primary staff who handled that sort of thing. Tyler had said it was important for interns to attend such meetings when Hampstead allowed it, and this was one of those times, three days after Ellie had taken coffee to her.

The gathering was scheduled for a conference room just past Hampstead's office, and Ellie was early. The door to the conference room stood slightly ajar and as Ellie entered, she almost ran into Hampstead, who was on her way out.

"Excuse me," Ellie said with a professional smile as she stepped aside, noting that Hampstead held a small flip phone in her hand. "I didn't realize anyone else was here."

"Ms. Daniels," Hampstead said by way of greeting, but she didn't move and instead she fixed Ellie with a gaze that made Ellie forget, momentarily, why she was there.

"Ma'am," Ellie said after a few moments, acutely aware that her heart rate was up and not because Hampstead had startled her.

Hampstead didn't respond and instead moved past her into the corridor and walked briskly toward the lobby. Ellie watched her and wondered why the hell someone like Hampstead would be carrying a flip phone. She'd been using a smartphone on the elevator earlier that week, and even if she carried more than one phone, why the outdated tech?

Unless it was a burn phone, which raised an interesting question. Why would Marya Hampstead need one? If she were carrying on some kind of illicit affair, why wouldn't she just use another smartphone for all her affairs? And why at the office, if it was something shady? Unless it was some kind of emergency in the something shady realm.

Ellie settled into a chair. Usually, people who tried to stay on the down-low used burn phones. They went for cheap ones with minimal function that were easy to carry and easy to get rid of. Like a flip phone. Ellie got up and went to the lobby, where another beautiful receptionist was working the desk.

"Hi," Ellie said to her. "Have you seen Ms. Hampstead? There's a meeting in a few minutes."

"She's out by the elevators," she said. "She'll be back in time. She always is."

"Good to know. I was just wanting to get a cup of coffee."

"Oh," the receptionist said with a conspiratorial smile. "You've got time."

Ellie checked the time on her phone. The meeting was slated to start in five minutes. She went into the coffee room, which was empty, and fired off a quick text to Rick about the possible burn phone and to see if Marya went outside to use it. She returned to the reception desk. "There's a line," she fibbed. "I'll wait here a couple of minutes."

The receptionist was on the phone, and she gave her a nod and another smile.

Four minutes. Ellie pretended to check her phone but she had positioned herself so that she could watch the elevators through the glass doors of the Fashion Forward lobby. Marya was not even interested in getting on the elevators. She stood near them, her back to the Fashion Forward offices, talking on her flip phone. The conversation ended, and Marya turned back toward the offices. Ellie went into the coffee room and texted Rick to let him know the target had not left the floor.

She returned to the conference room, carrying her phone as if she was checking something on it. A few others were already there, and several magazine layouts were positioned precisely in the middle of the table. Ellie offered a "hi" before she re-seated herself where she'd left her folders and tablet.

Tyler came in and greeted everyone before he sat next to her, putting himself between her and the head of the table. "How are things? I haven't gotten a chance to check in with you," he said.

"So far, so good. Liz has been really helpful, though some things are a little overwhelming."

"In what sense?"

"There's just a lot going on," she said, to alleviate his worried expression. "I guessed there would be, but when you really see the industry working through a place like this, it's so much more than anything you might have imagined."

He relaxed and smiled as a few other people came in. He greeted them by name and introduced her, though she figured nobody would remember her. Which was fine, since the less people remembered about her, the better.

The table filled up with one exception. Hampstead came in just as the clock on Ellie's phone registered the exact time that the meeting was supposed to start. She sat down.

"Look at this," she said without preliminaries as she pushed a button on a remote. One of the young women at the table had another remote and when she pressed hers, the lights dimmed and an image appeared on the screen against the opposite wall. It showed a magazine layout that was what Ellie would have called sleek with just a touch of grunge.

"*Mix* just hired a new design director who clearly is not afraid to take chances," Hampstead continued. "And there is no way in hell we are taking second to them."

The other woman with a remote turned the lights back up. Did Hampstead choreograph everything in her life? Was she never spontaneous? Regardless, she looked really good in her skirt. She probably looked even better out of it.

"Ideas. Now," Hampstead said.

A couple of pretty boys made suggestions about changing fonts on certain pages into something like *Mix* but Hampstead shut them down with a cool gaze.

"Tyler," Hampstead said, turning her gaze to him.

"I know the new guy at *Mix*. He used to do posters for indie bands back in the day, and he also worked as a promoter. So he's going for a rock n' roll kind of feel, and given the spring lines they'll be featuring, it fits. That's not us. We need to stay classic but with a few little tweaks here and there. Maybe a bit playful. A little bolder."

He clearly had a different relationship with her than the others gathered around the table. Tyler served as the royal advisor, while everybody else was a mere acolyte.

"Ms. Daniels?" Hampstead said, still looking at Tyler. The room seemed to hold its collective breath.

"Agent Carter," Ellie said. It was the first thing that popped into her head, and it seemed to take even Hampstead aback, because she raised her eyebrows.

"Meaning what, exactly?" Hampstead asked.

"Does anyone here watch the TV series?" Ellie continued. She was met with a couple of smiles from the other side of the table and a few nods. Hampstead's expression remained utterly unreadable. "Okay," Ellie continued, "what about evoking something like that? Kind of a bold forties retro thing with a palette that's both muted and splashy, like the comics and the show." Oh, my God. Had she just said that? Ellie fought a laugh at how ridiculous that sounded.

Tyler broke the silence. "I like it. There's something to it."

"Here." Ellie pulled up an image that featured the character wearing a red fedora and pointing a gun. She handed him her phone.

"Striking," Tyler said. "Bold. But still classic and classy." He took the phone to Hampstead, who studied the image for a long moment while he waited. Ellie watched Hampstead's fingers, wrapped around her phone. She had great hands.

Hampstead handed the phone back to him, and he passed it to Ellie as he took his seat.

"Other ideas?" Hampstead asked, sitting like she was on a throne.

A few brave souls offered tentative ideas about positioning of different elements on certain pages keyed to fonts and other graphic touches. Hampstead allowed it to go on for another fifteen minutes, and then she raised her hand. That's all it took. Everybody shut up. Ellie glanced at the clock on her phone. Thirty minutes on the money.

"Thank you, all," she said and almost on one accord, everyone got up, including Tyler. Ellie was a second late to stand because she didn't know the protocol until just then. Most started to leave, but Tyler lingered.

"Set a meeting up with design," Hampstead said to him. "No later than tomorrow afternoon."

"Already done. We're on for eleven. It should be on your calendar."

And that's why he was the royal advisor. Ellie moved past him toward the door, figuring Hampstead would want to plot world fashion domination with him.

"Thanks, Ellie," Tyler said.

She smiled. "Thanks to both of you for letting me attend." Oh, hell, yes. She had this acolyte speak *down*. Next stop, state dinners. Hampstead caught her gaze. Unreadable on the surface, but there was definitely something beneath. Lots of things. And they all made Ellie feel like she had a campfire low in her belly, and even lower than that. Uh-oh. She definitely had the hots for a target.

But damn, who could blame her? Hampstead was like Helen of Troy. A little scarier, but oh, so delicious.

"Agent Carter," Ellie muttered under her breath as she headed toward the coffee room. Now Hampstead would remember her as the crazy intern, thus making her job that much harder to gather information. Or, better yet, Hampstead would dismiss her as yet another dumbass intern and think nothing more of her.

Somehow, Ellie doubted that. Nothing got past Hampstead, and that might pose a big problem.

CHAPTER 5

"Did you talk to your UK people?" Ellie asked around the piece of candy in her mouth as she talked to Rick on the phone. She paused and leaned against a nearby building. She was really early today, and Fashion Forward was two blocks away.

"Waiting to hear back from a couple, but the other ones hadn't heard anything. They like the angle, and they're checking with some of their connections."

"If he's playing arms dealer and brokering hits, that would explain why the Petrovs are chasing him around."

"The question still remains, why those three guys in particular? Could be Daddy Koslov just asked Hampstead to look into the deaths, using his contacts. He probably deals with international intrigue all the time, so maybe that's the deal."

"Fine. Ruin my thriller, dude." She unwrapped another piece of candy.

Rick snorted a laugh. "Okay, I have to check with another precinct about a small-time crook they hauled in. He might be a Petrov. Maybe we can get something out of him if that's the case."

"Oh, sure. You get all the exciting assignments while I'm stuck in a high-rise office all day with fashion-obsessed people."

"Spare me, Els. Marya Hampstead is very easy on the eyes. And I'm sure if it came down to it, you wouldn't kick any of those beautiful people out of bed."

Ellie chewed the last bit of the candy, thinking about the way Hampstead's blouses fit her. "Whatever," she said after a pause.

"And the fact that you had to think about it just then is my proof. I'll check in with you later."

"Fine," she said, irritated. This case was still going nowhere. She'd been interning for almost two weeks, and with the exception of the flip phone incident, Marya Hampstead hadn't done anything to suggest she was on the take with an international arms dealer. Unless she was just that good at it. Hiding in plain sight, as a celebrity. That was brazen, but if it was true, she sort of admired Marya for it, though she still thought the key to this whole thing was Marya's dad.

Ellie dropped her phone into her shoulder bag as she walked. She would be at Fashion Forward twenty minutes early, and when she entered the building's massive lobby, the digital clock at the security counter proved her right.

She walked toward the elevators, her heels clicking on the marble. If nothing else, she'd gotten really good walking in shoes like these. Her fashion consultant had granted her a light gray pantsuit today, with another fitted but masculine-cut shirt in white and, much to Ellie's delight, a slim black tie to match her black heels. The maroon flaps on the pockets of her blazer gave her the "edgy factor" the consultant kept talking about.

Ellie had almost made it to the elevators when she heard her name in an all-too-familiar voice. No time to run. And she'd probably look crazed if she tried to while dressed like this. She turned, steeling herself.

"Oh, hey. Hi, Gwen." Really? Her ex here in the Fashion Forward building?

"I thought that was you. Hi."

Before Ellie could prepare, Gwen gave her a quick hug.

"You look really nice," Gwen said as she stepped back.

"Thanks. So do you." But Gwen always looked good. Today's power suit was a sleek blue that matched her eyes. She wore a very classy off-white blouse, and it amused Ellie that she knew the blouse was silk just by looking at it. Only two weeks at Fashion Forward and look at her now.

"Hello," said the guy standing to Gwen's right. His power suit was a light green, cut in a slim line that fit him really well, along with a classic light blue pinstripe shirt with a dark blue tie.

Gwen introduced the guy with her, then said, "This is Ellie—"

"Daniels," Ellie said smoothly, cutting Gwen off. "Nice to meet you." Gwen frowned, but didn't say anything, fortunately. "So what brings you two here?"

"We have an appointment with a client," Gwen said.

"Ah. Well, we can ride up together." Ellie smiled. "Come on." She should win an Oscar for this performance. She continued to the elevator, hoping Gwen would suddenly be called away to the other side of New York on more important business. She pressed the button, dreading how long they'd have to wait.

"So—" Gwen started.

"Ms. Daniels," another voice said.

Oh, God. Ellie hadn't seen Marya approach since she'd been focused on getting through the next few minutes with Gwen. "Ms. Hampstead." She offered her most professional smile. She recognized the two men with her, but she didn't know their names. They smiled at her and murmured greetings.

"Gwen," Marya said with a smile. She took her sunglasses off. "It's been a while. How are you?"

Ellie tried to make it look like she wasn't staring, but she was sure it wasn't working.

"I'm well, thank you. I saw your latest projects are bringing some well-deserved accolades. Kudos to you and your staff."

"We do try," Marya said with another smile, and Ellie forced herself not to look at Marya's lips because when she smiled, it made them that much more inviting. How much more awkward could this get? And since when did Marya smile? At Ellie's ex, no less?

Marya turned to Ellie. "Gwen's law firm handled a situation we had a few months ago. Gwen, this is Ellie Daniels. She's doing an internship with us." She ignored Gwen's colleague, who seemed to grasp that this was a woman you really didn't want to mess with.

"We've met," Ellie said, giving Gwen another one of her professional smiles, hoping Gwen wouldn't blow her cover.

"Yes," Gwen said with an answering professional smile. "Different circumstances. Just a coincidence, running into each other here."

The elevator dinged, and the door opened, disgorging several passengers. Ellie wanted to throw herself inside and kiss the floor because there would be at least ten other people riding up with her and she wouldn't have to talk to either Gwen or Marya.

The elevator did fill up, but Ellie ended up between Marya and Gwen. The gods were not smiling on her this day. Perhaps it was penance for smacking Yuri Laskin with Gwen's blender, though you'd think they'd appreciate it, given Laskin's history.

"So how do you two know each other?" Marya asked, and Ellie wasn't sure which surprised her more, the question itself or the fact that Marya Hampstead, ice queen, had asked it. And so help her, God, but Marya looked amazing. She wore a blouse the color of some ritzy red wine and herringbone pants and matching jacket. The latter had a cool military cut to it, like one of those World War II short uniform jackets soldiers wore, and her collar was open to expose an understated silver necklace with a small pendant that held a black stone.

"We met at a fundraising event a while back," Gwen said, giving Ellie a pointed look. "We stayed in touch."

Ellie silently thanked Gwen. And it was a true story, so Gwen didn't have to lie. She'd have to have lunch with her now.

"And how did you come to intern with Marya?" Gwen asked Ellie, and Ellie silently cancelled the lunch.

"Pure chance. I saw the listing and applied. You know I've always wanted to get more involved in fashion publishing." She gave Gwen her own version of a pointed look. "Chasing a dream."

The elevator stopped at the twentieth floor before Gwen could say anything else and several people got out. One of Marya's assistants held the door open as Gwen and her colleague worked their way out.

"Good to see you," Marya said to Gwen. "I'll contact you later. If you have some time this week, perhaps we can catch up."

"I'd like that." Gwen stepped off the elevator. "Don't be a stranger," she said to Ellie as the doors closed.

Catch up? Ellie's ex and Marya Hampstead? What the hell? Still eleven floors to go. And still shoved in tight next to Marya. So tight that their arms were touching, and Ellie was afraid the heat level within her would seep through her clothes and Marya would feel it. So not cool to be this attracted to a target. So not cool at all. The elevator stopped again and a few more people got off, which allowed Ellie to move away from Marya, who appeared to be scrolling through email on her phone.

Finally, the elevator arrived at the floor for Fashion Forward. Ellie waited for Marya and her boys to get off first before she headed for the coffee, though she would've liked something stronger.

"Ms. Daniels," Marya said, and Ellie turned, maintaining a perfect professional veneer. "That's a good look on you." Marya tugged on her own collar to indicate the tie, and then continued through the lobby. One of her boys stared curiously at Ellie for another few seconds.

Seriously? Marya Hampstead just complimented her outfit? Ellie went to get a cup of coffee, wondering what the ice queen had up her sleeve. When she got to her office, she fired off a text to Gwen: "Good to see you. Working a case. Catch up with you later." There. That was nice enough. Liz wasn't at her desk, but the cup of coffee on her desk was steaming, and there was a stack of layouts on Ellie's desk to proofread. Good thing she did have an eye for that.

She sat down and started going through the layouts, trying to concentrate, but she kept thinking about Gwen and then Marya. Awkward, to be sandwiched between her ex and a woman she kind of had a crush on, who may or may not be dealing international arms—hello. What was this? Ellie stared at the photo, a full-page shot of a model doing the catwalk thing. The photo credit said "Nadia Koslov."

"Oh, hi," Liz said as she entered. She put another batch of layouts on her desk.

"Hi. Who's this?" Ellie pointed at the photo.

Liz leaned over. "Oh, that's Natalie Koslov. She goes by Nadia professionally, though."

"Koslov?"

"Yeah. She's not Russian, though. Well, I mean, she is, but she was born here, so she's a US citizen. She has a lot of family in the city and in Russia."

Of course she does. "What's her connection to Fashion Forward?" Ellie asked, trying to sound mildly curious. "I haven't seen her in any of the other layouts."

"Besides the fact that Ms. Hampstead knows everybody in the industry?" Liz asked with a smile.

Ellie smiled back. "Dumb question, right?"

"Well, some models do get more play here. Natalie's one of them. Ms. Hampstead likes her attitude." Liz shrugged. "She uses her images quite a bit."

"Do you know her?"

"Natalie?"

Ellie nodded.

"No, but she comes around. I've seen her a few times in Marya's office. A couple weeks ago. Like, the Wednesday before you started work here. I think she's a cousin of that guy who sometimes hangs around Ms. Hampstead. Lyev? I think that's his name."

Thank you, Liz, Ellie thought. "Cool. Maybe someday I'll be able to sling names around like you."

Liz laughed and sat down at her own desk. They worked in silence for a while until Liz put her phone on a nearby speaker and streamed some innocuous pop music. Ellie waited a few more minutes before she ran a basic web search on Nadia Koslov. Pretty well known on the circuit, it looked like. She even had her own website. Ellie glanced at Liz, who was engrossed in her own stack of layouts, and clicked on the appearances page on Koslov's site. And how interesting. She was doing a show this Saturday, the day after tomorrow, in the city. Sponsored by Fashion Forward.

A knock sounded on the office door and both looked up as it opened.

"Hey," Tyler said. "Do you have a minute, Ellie?"

"Sure." She stepped out of the office.

"So I've got a great opportunity for you," he said. "But there's a catch."

"There always is. What is it?"

"I need someone to be a gopher at a fashion show. It's not the best work, and people can be bitchy, but you'll get to see how it works on the ground."

"What's the catch?" Ellie asked.

"Besides the bitchy?"

"That goes with the territory," she said with a smile.

He laughed. "True. I see you're learning how things work. The catch is, it's Saturday."

Oh, hell, yes. "I'm in."

He smiled again, this time with obvious relief. "Thank you so much. I'll warn you now that it gets a little hectic at a show, even though most of the stuff we do for Fashion Week is already over."

"Just tell me what you want me to do."

"Thanks. Stop by my office around four today, and I'll give you some tips. I won't be around much tomorrow, since I'll be busy at the venue."

"Okay. Thanks for the invite."

"Oh, and, wear something similar to what you have on. It's a great look on you." He hurried away, but called back over his shoulder, "And wear comfortable shoes."

That was good news. She could be a little more butch and get away with it, and she was for sure ditching the heels on Saturday, no matter what her consultant said. Ellie went back into her office and returned to looking at layouts, and then she went online and called up twelve months of back issues of every Fashion Forward publication. She sent the links to Rick and told him to get with the IT people and run searches for Russian models— especially ones that worked regularly with the house of Hampstead. She included the link to Natalie Koslov's website and told him to run down everything he could find on her.

Could be a coincidence, a Koslov in the model stable. And since Natalie was related to Lyev, it could be Lyev helped her get a job in the industry, and introduced her to Marya. But it seemed a little *too* coincidental.

Liz got up with a stack of layouts. "More coffee?" she asked.

"That'd be great. Italian roast, a little bit of cream."

"Okay." Liz left, and Ellie dug into her purse for another cinnamon candy. She was running low. Should've bought some at lunch. While Liz was gone, she ran some searches trying to determine why Gwen might've been involved with Fashion Forward. Nothing showed up, but Ellie wasn't surprised. Marya kept a tight lid on company business, and Gwen did the same. Which meant Ellie would have to ask Gwen personally, especially if there were no records of whatever the matter was. If it didn't get to court and if there were no formal charges, there wouldn't be any paper trail in public documents.

She sighed. She'd have to find out, to rule it out as relevant to the current investigation. Her phone alerted her to a text message and Ellie picked it up. This was a coincidence she did believe in. Gwen, responding to her earlier text. She apologized for putting Ellie on the spot, but it was unexpected to see her there.

"Yeah, yeah," Ellie muttered. She texted Gwen back and asked if she could call her later that evening.

Gwen responded almost immediately in the affirmative along with a time. Lawyers. Ellie rolled her eyes but smiled. She texted "okay, great" back and set her phone down. Hopefully, Marya's legal situation had nothing to do with the case. Because it would really suck to have to drag Gwen into this.

She went back to proofreading the layouts since Tyler had requested them before the end of the day. Most likely, Marya had delegated that to him, which meant Marya wanted to see them by the end of the day, and the last thing Ellie wanted to do was get on the dragon lady's bad side. Or rather, worse side.

Liz came back in and handed her a cup of coffee. A few minutes later, they were both engrossed in their tasks, though Ellie hoped that the team would be able to dig some stuff up on the models. She had a feeling there was something going on there, but until she had more information, she wasn't sure how to proceed. For now, she'd continue to bide her time.

The door to Tyler's office was partially open, but Ellie knocked anyway.

"Come in," he said, and she stepped into the office. He was sitting at his desk, which was covered with glossy photos of models in various runway poses. "Oh, hi," he said when he saw her. "Is it four already?"

"Five 'til. I can come back."

"No, no. Sit down." He smiled and motioned at the chairs across from his desk.

She did, and he must have caught her looking at the photos, because he said, "Publicity stills. People like to get signed photos of the models—especially the more well-known ones. That's one of the things you'll be doing on

Saturday, is making sure photos are available for signing. Since we're past the crazy that is Fashion Week, the models have agreed to do some autographs."

"Signing before or after the runway?"

"After. And then there's a cocktail reception near the venue." He clicked a few things on his computer, and the printer started to whir. "Here." He handed her the two sheets of paper the printer ejected. "Outline of how this is going to work tomorrow."

She took the sheets and glanced through them. "So basically, this is one of those be-available-but-unobtrusive things."

He laughed. "I do like how you distill things to the essence. Yes, that's it. And Marya does allow staff to attend the reception afterward, and no, you don't have to work it. She believes in working hard and then relaxing a bit."

Really? Marya Hampstead relaxes?

At her expression, he smiled. "Yes, the rumors about Marya Hampstead can be true, but she also recognizes the value of treating staff well when they earn it." He smoothed his tie, an extremely stylish metallic blue in a thin cut, like what men wore in the sixties and like what Ellie was wearing now.

Interesting choice of words: "Can be" true. So Marya wasn't always a dragon lady. Ellie skimmed the sheets of paper again.

"The seating has already been arranged, so you won't have to deal with that or escorting anyone."

"Okay."

"I'll let you know if that changes, but I doubt it. Don't worry about it. Just ask for Liz at the venue Saturday.

And I'll be there, of course, so you can always find me with questions. My cell phone number is on the first page, but when you arrive tomorrow, you'll get a headset, which is the best way to communicate at these events—have you used them before?"

If he only knew. "Yeah. A while ago," she fibbed.

"They're easy. And they're lightweight and come with clips, so you won't have to worry about taking it off your jacket or belt or whatever constantly. Just click and talk."

"Wow. I guess I never really thought about all that goes into doing an event like this. Is it true that the big names get the front seats?"

"Yes. Those are known celebrities and people of influence, as I call them. So you may not recognize some, but if they're in the first row, that's what they are."

"Is there some kind of orientation session before I do this?"

"Sometimes. Not really for this. Fashion Weeks definitely. But this show isn't that big, and I figured you'd want to experience this before your internship ends, so I'm squeezing you in, and we'll guide you through. Besides, I think you can handle it." His cell phone rang, and he glanced at it and then looked at her, apologetic. "I'll be around part of the day tomorrow. I'll check in with you in the morning."

"Sounds good. Thanks."

He nodded and answered his phone. Ellie got up and stepped into the hallway, leaving his door like she'd found it.

"Hey, Ellie."

"Hi," she said to Khalil, who really liked bowties, clearly. The one he had on today was burgundy with small white dots, and it looked really good with his pewter-colored shirt. Ellie winced internally that she was actually assessing people's clothes and color schemes. "Tyler's on the phone," she said since it appeared Khalil was waiting to talk to him.

"I figured." He held a bunch of papers and photographs. "Things get crazy before a show."

"So I see." She was about to say something else when he looked past her shoulder and straightened.

"Waiting on Tyler, Ms. H."

Ellie turned, steeling herself for what she knew would be the extremely attractive sight of Marya. "Ms. Daniels," she said in greeting.

"Ma'am." Ellie nodded once.

Marya seemed to be studying her again, but Ellie met and held her gaze, and it was delicious. Ellie's thighs felt like they might burst into flame.

Tyler opened his door wider. "Okay. I'm off the phone."

Marya broke the moment with Ellie to look at him as Khalil brushed past them to go into Tyler's office. Marya looked back at Ellie, the hint of a smile gracing the corners of her mouth. "Ma'am," Marya said, as if trying the word out for the first time. "That's the second time you've called me that." The smile unfurled a little, sparking in her eyes, and Ellie wondered if her entire body would burst into flame.

"Do I truly strike you as that?" Marya regarded her, nothing beyond interest in her tone.

"Now that you mention it, no," Ellie said.

"Good." Her gaze seared into Ellie's again, that damn Mona Lisa smile hovering on her mouth. And then she entered Tyler's office and shut the door, leaving Ellie in the hallway, burning in places she didn't know she had. She went back to her office, and it occurred to her that Marya had remembered the other time Ellie had called her "ma'am." She shut her computer down and gathered her things.

CHAPTER 6

Ellie dropped her bag onto the floor and collapsed on the couch. It hadn't been broken in by anybody sleeping or sitting on it for hours at a time, so it was still a little stiff, but she was tired and didn't care. And she was also tired of takeout, but she hadn't had time to get any real food for this apartment.

She did have beer in the fridge, so she rolled off the couch and retrieved a bottle. Ellie watched the clock on her phone. Gwen, like Marya, preferred appointments to be right on the agreed-upon time. The thought made Ellie wonder if she had some kind of weird thing for uptight women.

Seven o'clock showed on her phone, so she called Gwen and sank back down on the couch and put her feet on the coffee table.

"Hi," Gwen answered. "Good to see you today," she said, getting right to the point.

"Yeah, sorry about all this. I'm on assignment and clearly didn't expect to run into you."

She laughed. "I know I can't ask you the particulars, but I will say that you look fabulous. I almost wish you'd dressed like that more often when we were together."

Ellie smiled as she took a drink. "Thanks, I think. Anyway, no, I can't really tell you the particulars, but unfortunately, I have to ask you about the legal matter you handled for Marya Hampstead."

Silence. Uh-oh.

"You know I can't discuss cases or clients," Gwen finally said, in her quiet professional tone.

Double uh-oh. Another wall had just gone up. "I get that, but this is an active investigation, and I just want to make sure that whatever the legal matter was, it has nothing to do with what I'm doing."

"Which is what, exactly?"

Triple uh-oh. Time to hedge. "Okay, fine. Because it's you and nobody else, we're looking into clothing knock-offs out of China, and we got some complaints from some of the higher-ups in the fashion industry. We're trying to figure out who might be bringing them into the country. Fashion Forward is letting us borrow them as a staging area. And you did not hear that from me. I will deny everything. So will they." Oh, my God. Best lie ever. She should do improv.

"Oh," Gwen said, and Ellie could hear the relief behind it. "No, this was about a contract dispute with an overseas modeling agency."

"Good to know," Ellie said, with her own obvious relief. "So how exactly did you get involved in that? I didn't realize you were attorney to the fashion industry. Or is that a new development?"

"Nothing like that. I met Marya at a fundraising gala in June—I seem to meet a lot of people that way—and I was introduced as an attorney. She requested my card, which I provided, not thinking much about it. A few days later she called and asked if I might consider helping them with the dispute."

Marya no doubt did some research on Gwen before she called. And June was good. That was almost eight months after Ellie and Gwen had split up, so Marya would have no reason to associate the two of them together. "Any particular reason she called you, out of all the attorneys who were probably at that gala?"

Silence. Shit.

"Jesus, El. Will you stop being a cop for once?"

Ellie started to retort, then realized that was a bad idea. "I'm sorry," she said instead. "That was out of line." She grimaced and took another swallow of beer.

"Yes, it was. And apology accepted. But since you asked, I'm guessing her board probably suggested it, since I know two people on it and one of them introduced us at the gala. I do corporate contracts and issues all the time. It's not that far afield to handle something like this, and as it turned out, it was easily dealt with and settled and everybody's happy."

"Congratulations. If only they were all that simple."

Gwen chuckled. "Right? So how are you otherwise?"

She stifled a sigh. Gwen wasn't trying to pry. She cared, and it always made Ellie uncomfortable, that someone would. Especially an ex. "Okay. Pretty busy."

"And?"

"Nothing much else to tell."

"How's your family?"

"Fine."

"El, it's me. It's okay to talk to me, even though we're not partners anymore. I would like to be a friend. And that's what friends do. They talk."

Ellie set her empty bottle on the coffee table. "I know you're right, but I guess I still have a hard time—you know."

"Opening up. And again, you used to talk about this stuff with me. I'm still me. You're still you. I still care about you, and I still like you. And you haven't hung up yet, which means you do want to talk."

Dammit. She was right. Ellie stretched out on the couch and stared at the ceiling, a generic white like practically every motel in America, which was how this place felt. Impersonal and bland. "Okay. Mom's fine. She started taking pottery classes, and she's loving it so far."

"Seriously?"

"Yeah. You know she's always been into crafts. I just really hope she doesn't get so into it that she inundates me with crazy-shaped cups and bowls."

Gwen laughed again. "Maybe she'll give them to your sister instead."

"She'll probably give them to us both. And the cousins. Probably Gran, too. We'll have so much damn pottery we'll be able to have a booth at a flea market, doing the local art thing. And look out. You might get a set for Christmas."

"I'll treasure it always," Gwen said, still laughing.

"Yeah, well, you've been warned." And Ellie realized it was actually nice to talk to her like this. Having a shared past meant they'd already gotten through a lot of the bullshit small talk. "So how are things with your folks?"

"They still argue about where to take their next vacation. And they do still ask about you."

"That's kind of sweet."

"They like you, El. No big surprise. You're actually really likable when you're not—"

"Being an asshole cop."

"Not quite my word choice, but close." She laughed.

"I seem to not be able to turn that off all the time."

"Goes with the territory. The same could be said for me and asshole lawyers."

"No comment."

"Hey, now. I do try to turn it off."

Ellie chuckled. "I know. I'm still working on mine."

"I'm glad. Speaking of the cop thing, as a tip, Marya's not what you think."

"Uh..." What the hell?

"That is, she has a rep, but it's mostly for show."

"Okay. And that means what, exactly?" Please, Gwen, don't be running arms deals with Marya, Ellie chanted in her head.

"Just don't put too much stock in what you hear."

"So rumors of her asshole status are exaggerated. Good to know." She took another swallow of beer.

"The point is, I rather like Marya, so whatever you're doing over there, please try not to be *too* cop."

Ellie laughed. "Seriously? Are you warning me or are you trying to help me?"

"Maybe a bit of both. She can be an excellent ally. It might be good to have her as that."

"Noted. Thanks for the tip. Not that cops and fashion ever mix."

"Start thinking in terms of allies rather than adversaries," Gwen said, cryptic. "And I have to go. I've got a thing tonight. Thanks for talking. And don't worry. Your last name is Daniels until you tell me otherwise."

"Which reminds me—can you do me a favor and not hang out with Marya for, like, a month or so?"

"Oh. You probably have a manufactured story about your past for this internship." She said it as a statement. Gwen was all too familiar with how some of Ellie's past ops had gone down.

"Yeah. Sorry about that."

"It's your job. I'll be careful."

"Thanks. I really appreciate that. And maybe I am ready to have lunch with you. Or coffee."

"I would love that," she said, and Ellie heard her smile.

"Okay. Keep in touch. And take care."

"You too. Bye."

Ellie hung up. That wasn't so bad. Except for lying about what the investigation actually was, but it was a small lie in the great scheme of things, and it protected everybody. There were days, however, when she didn't like the lying, so when this was over, she'd square it with Gwen. She set her phone on the coffee table and shut her eyes for a moment, trying to chill out after what had been kind of an emotionally weird day. She mulled what Gwen had said about Marya. That added to the weirdness. So maybe Marya wasn't an ice queen? At least not all the time? Well, so what? Not like it mattered, when all was said and done. She relaxed, pondering the case.

Her phone rang, but it sounded like it was far away. Ellie jerked and looked around. What the hell? Shit, she'd fallen asleep, and her phone was both buzzing and ringing. Finally, she realized it was Rick.

"Hey," she answered. "What's up?" She rubbed her eyes, trying to sound more awake than she felt.

"You dressed?"

"Uh—"

"You're going to a club."

Ellie was now fully awake. "What?"

"A club. Dancing. You."

"Dude, I don't do that shit anymore."

"You are tonight. Marya and her entourage are at Lucky in SoHo right now. I've got a car on the way to get you."

"Why—"

"Lyev Koslov was seen going in a few minutes after Hampstead, and that was ten minutes ago."

Ellie was off the couch and heading for her closet. "So what's the play? Am I going in as Daniels?" She slid the closet door open and examined her wardrobe, which had been greatly enhanced recently.

"Yes. And you'll have company. Sue will meet you there. Be ready in fifteen."

"Damn, you don't give a woman much time to get ready. Maybe that's why you're having a hard time dating."

"Maybe I'll switch to dating lesbians."

"Ha, ha. Some of us are into the primp city thing. I'm not one of them, but I know some."

"Fourteen minutes, Els. Out."

He hung up, and Ellie checked the clock on her phone. Almost ten-thirty. At least she'd gotten a nice nap. She tossed her phone on the bed and rummaged through the blouses and shirts. She selected one of her own, a black button-down in a man's cut, and a pair of soft grey trousers with tapered legs that looked really good with her black wingtips. She put her compression holster T-shirt on and slid her Glock into the pocket for it just under her left armpit and put the black shirt on over it. Whoever came up with these holster tees had her vote for president. They were form-fitting, and compressed the lines of the gun so it was really hard to tell if someone had one under a blouse, even if that person didn't have a jacket or blazer on.

She finished dressing and ran her fingers through her hair, which was growing out pretty nicely. Sort of a tousled carefree look that she never would have thought would look good on her, but it did. She completed her outfit with a slim-fitting black leather jacket. It was a club, after all.

Ellie doubted that Marya would be able to pick her out of a club crowd. She wouldn't be expecting her there, so even if Marya spotted her, Ellie was out of context and dressed differently than at work. That was her theory, anyway, but Marya was observant, so her theory might be out the window. She spritzed on some cologne, checked her hair one more time, and stepped out of the apartment into the interior hallway of the building. After she locked up, she went downstairs to wait for her ride. Maybe they'd finally get a break in this damn case.

CHAPTER 7

"Aren't you a sight for sore eyes," Sue said when Ellie stepped out of the car onto the curb. "I'd almost go lesbian for you."

"Almost?" She grinned at her. The driver had dropped her off a couple of blocks from the club, and Sue was standing outside a Chinese restaurant waiting for her. It smelled good, and she remembered that she hadn't eaten dinner yet. Hell, at this rate, she should probably just wait until breakfast.

"If I was single, it might be another matter." Sue pretended to fan herself.

"You're not so bad yourself." Ellie gave her a once-over, and she laughed. She was petite, but a complete badass and had thrown men twice her size to the mat in training. Tonight she'd let her dark hair hang free without her usual ponytail. She was wearing black pants and a burgundy blouse underneath a white blazer that fit her curves nicely. Ellie guessed she'd picked white so Ellie could find her in the crowd.

"Don't I know it. Let's go, stud." Sue started walking.

"Shut up, Morales."

"You love it."

She laughed. "So what's the situation?" she asked as they headed to the club.

"Hampstead had dinner with her entourage and then took a cab to Lucky. Lyev Koslov pulled up in a private car about fifteen minutes later."

"Did he go in alone?" She dodged a group of people laughing and not paying much attention to their surroundings.

"No. Two women were with him who look like they play for the Swedish national volleyball team."

"Does Sweden even have a volleyball team?"

"Do you not pay attention to women's sports? I thought all lesbians did."

"That's a stereotype."

"Spare me. These two women should front that team." She stopped abruptly and took her phone out of her pocketbook. "Texting you the photo of him and his company that surveillance grabbed."

Ellie's phone vibrated in the inside pocket of her jacket.

"In the meantime, here." Sue handed her phone over and Ellie checked the photo. Koslov was dressed in what looked like a black suit, but it could've been navy, given the distance the photo was taken from. Sue was right. The two women he was with easily could've been six feet tall each, though he still had a couple of inches on them. Both were dressed in slinky evening dresses, one black and the other red.

"They're probably models. And Koslov is living up to his playboy rep, I see." She handed the phone back, and Sue returned it to her pocketbook as she resumed walking.

"Or just living up to the act."

"Or that."

They crossed a street, and the club wasn't too far ahead. There wasn't much of a line, but that didn't mean anything because it wasn't yet eleven-thirty. Within an hour, the line would be much longer. Two bouncers stood at the entrance, dressed in suits. They probably had to have them custom-made, because these dudes were huge. She handed the driver's license for Ellie Daniels over to the one checking. He looked at it, looked at her, and handed it back. She waited for Sue to go through the same process, and they entered.

Lucky was designed to evoke a 1920s-era speakeasy, and the décor and color schemes lent themselves to that. A bar ran almost the entire length of the back wall of the front room, bottles stacked on glass shelves behind it. Café tables dotted the room, and the chairs looked like they were modeled on the era, as well. The dance floor was in another room, and the thump-thump-thump of house music filtered through the wall.

"Club soda okay?" Sue said near her ear.

"Yeah. With lime."

Sue moved toward the bar, and Ellie surveyed the room. Every seat at the bar was taken, and every table, too, but there was no sign of Marya or Koslov. She texted Rick and asked him if either of those two had snuck out the back.

A few seconds later her phone buzzed with his response, which was *no*.

She pretended to be checking her phone, but she scoped out the tables carefully. No sign of the targets. Sue handed her a glass, and she took a sip. Not bad, and it looked like it might be alcohol with the lime and the cherry in it.

"Anything?" Sue asked.

"No. Rick says they're still here, though."

"Let's check." Sue pushed through a group of guys taking up space next to the bar and went into the next room, which had more of an urban cool lounge vibe, with low couches and overstuffed chairs set strategically out of the way of foot traffic. The primary color scheme in here was shades of blue, black, and slashes of white. Track lighting kept it feeling warmer, however, and the music had an ambient vibe, but the thumping from the dance floor was still audible.

Sue ran her hand up Ellie's arm and placed it on the back of her neck.

"Play along with me, girl," she said as she pulled her closer with her one hand while she held her drink with the other. "Looks like a bunch of your people are in here."

Ellie almost spit her drink out with her laugh. "My people?"

"Definitely a Sapphic vibe," Sue said, breath warm on her cheek as she continued to pretend to be sharing an intimate moment with her.

"Sapphic? Really? Who have you been hanging out with?"

She giggled and stroked Ellie's neck with her thumb and moved against her like they were dancing.

"Jesus, if there's an Oscar for something like this, I'm nominating you," she said next to Sue's ear.

"A lesbian and a straight woman walk into a bar," Sue said in a low voice.

"And then they went into the next room, looking for the targets," she responded, voice equally low. She took her hand and led them deeper into the club. She checked the crowd as they made their way, and Sue was right. There did seem to be a concentration of women in this room, and quite a few appeared to have brought female dates. She'd have to remember that about this place. That is, if she ever had another date and decided to go out.

All of which was questionable at the moment, though she knew who she'd like to have a date with.

She squeezed past people who had congregated just on the other side of the doorway into the third room. A smaller bar than the first room was on the opposite wall, and this area had a few more tables set up. The dance floor had to be in the next room, because the thump-thump-thump seeped up through the floor and into her body. And yes, there was the doorway that would take you there. Lights flashed from it. Not much of a chance that she or Sue would be able to overhear anybody's conversation unless they were right next to whoever was talking, but they could at least try for some photos.

"Let's split up," Sue said near her ear.

She nodded and let go of her hand to slowly work her way toward the back of the room, holding her drink close to prevent it from getting bumped. She made it to a corner without spotting anybody when her phone vibrated in her pocket. She leaned against a wall, out of the way of people, and checked it. Sue had texted a message: *Swede at back corner table over here.*

Swede. She laughed. Koslov's dates probably weren't even Swedish. She texted back. *On my way.* As she navigated through the crowd, she finished her drink, pushed to the bar, and left the glass there before maneuvering her way to the opposite side of the room where she spotted Sue's white blazer. Once next to her, Sue acted like she was really happy to see her and positioned them for a selfie, which she took quickly. She showed her phone to Ellie and a few feet away sitting at a table was one of the women Koslov had come in with.

"Nice work," she said, leaning close so Sue could hear. "Where are our other friends?"

"Don't know. I'll check the women's room. Texted Rick to make sure they didn't leave," she said. "They haven't."

"All right. I'll check the dance floor." Although why the hell Hampstead would be doing that if she was trying to seal an arms deal with Koslov was beyond her, unless they were trying to keep up appearances. She put her phone back in her pocket.

The music slammed into her when she stepped through the doorway. The dance floor took up the center of the room, level with the rest of the floor. Probably a good thing, since trying to go up or down onto a dance floor at a club was hard enough when you hadn't been drinking. The DJ booth sat against the back wall, and lights spun and jerked in time with the beat. To the right of the booth, there was a black door that she guessed led outside. As she watched, the door opened and a guy carrying a box suddenly appeared. He kicked the door shut with his foot. So the door led to the storage area, and chances were, there was another door to the outside. The DJ bounced over to the door and propped it halfway open. Maybe she was able to get a breeze that way.

Ellie moved carefully around the periphery of the floor, scanning for Koslov. He was big, and she'd probably see him first. The music pounded through her shoes. As a cop, she hated venues like this because she couldn't hear anything and people moved quickly and bumped into others. Great place to pick a few pockets. She checked to make sure her phone, ID, and cash were still in her inside jacket pocket.

The song's beat changed slightly, and several more people pushed past her onto the dance floor. Christ, this was a bust. Nobody did arms deals on a dance floor. She tried to step back from the floor, but was hemmed in from behind. She stepped to the side, and the people dancing closest to her shifted to her right, and there was Koslov, right in the middle of the crowd, dancing with one of the women he'd shown up with. And though she only got a glimpse, right next to him was someone who looked a lot like Marya.

A hand on her arm made her tense up, until she realized it was Sue, who gestured at the floor and nodded, indicating she'd seen him, too. And then she did one of the worst things she could have done and pulled Ellie onto the floor with her.

"What the fuck," she mouthed at her, but Sue just grinned and started dancing, swaying seductively at her.

"C'mon, O'Donnell," she purred in her ear. "I know you can tear a floor up. I've seen it."

"I was drinking," Ellie shot back with a smile, but she pulled her close and started to move. Sue laughed, and the DJ slowed the beat to a slower groove and several more people hit the floor, pushing them closer to the middle.

"Damn, you've still got skills," Sue said as she put both arms around Ellie's neck. "Can I call you if I want to experiment?"

"Hell, no."

Sue giggled in her ear then maneuvered them around until Ellie almost bumped into Koslov. She was so glad Rick wasn't seeing this. He'd never let her hear the end of it. The beat picked up, and the crowd went with it, putting their hands in the air and whooping and hollering. Someone pushed into her back, and she tried to move to get out of the way. The crowd shifted again, and suddenly she was staring into the eyes of Marya Hampstead.

Oh, God. Busted. So busted.

Marya's eyebrows lifted in surprise, and Ellie smiled and offered a "fancy meeting you here" expression and then made a show of getting out of her way. Didn't mean to bump the dragon lady, she hoped her expression said. And it's a total coincidence that I'm here, she added silently. Nothing to see here. Move along. The crowd's arms shot up and people whooped again, and holy hellfire, Marya grabbed the lapels of her jacket and pulled her close.

What the fuck?

Marya Hampstead wanted to dance with her?

Was this even legal? There had to be a law against dancing with Marya Hampstead. Didn't people implode if they got this close to her? And wait a minute, why was Marya trying to dance with another woman?

The song slowed again, and Marya leaned in and said in her ear, "This is an even better look on you."

She managed a smile as the heat of Marya's breath sent chills all the way down her legs. "Thanks," she said, but Marya had released her lapels and was dancing with Koslov and his date again, as well as three guys from her entourage, who Ellie just noticed.

Sue suddenly appeared, still dancing, and gave her a full-on leer before she slipped her arms around her neck again and did another sexy groove against her. Ellie grooved right back. She was undercover, after all. Besides, she did enjoy dancing, though she didn't do it in public much. Sue was a good dancer and kept them next to Koslov, who wasn't too bad himself. Ellie glanced at him, then the woman he'd come with, and then she ran into Marya's gaze again.

And stayed there for what was much longer than proper. She finally looked away, but not before the hint of a smile quirked the corner of Marya's mouth. But she probably imagined it, right? She tried not to look at her again, but dammit, Marya knew how to move on a dance floor, knew how to work her hips, and yes, she was smiling a little and, good God, how could someone be that sexy without even trying?

Ellie focused on Sue. Marya Hampstead was hot incarnate, but she was also a potential arms dealer, and it was a very bad idea to lust after someone she'd probably have to bust later. Not to mention, she was her boss. Sort of. And probably straight. Oh, God, this was all kinds of messed up.

The song changed, and Koslov and his date started to leave the floor. Marya followed them, with a little nod at Ellie as she passed. Her entourage trailed after her.

"I'd go lesbian for her, too," Sue said in her ear.

"Probably this whole bar would. Let's see where they went."

Sue started moving through the crowd, keeping the beat as if she was just trying to find another place to dance. Ellie followed and finally, they were off the floor. Sue gripped her hand and pulled her into the adjoining room and toward the bar, like she wanted to order something.

Sue leaned in. "Koslov at your three."

Ellie looked to her right and sure enough, there he was, a few feet away, leaning down and talking to Marya, who was surrounded by her entourage. The body language between Marya and Koslov didn't suggest a physically intimate relationship, but then, they might just be fuck buddies or something. Marya probably had some other phrase for it, and it sounded sexy and classy when she said it. She went through her knowledge of British slang. Shag mates was the best she could come up with and that seemed unlikely.

Sue handed her a bottle of water, and she gratefully chugged it. She was sweating underneath her jacket.

"On the move," Sue said, and she looked up in time to see Koslov working his way through the crowd back toward the dance floor, both of the women he'd come with next to him.

"Where's Marya?" she asked.

"Don't know. Might be leaving." Sue was already texting, and Ellie guessed the message was to Rick. She grabbed Ellie and pulled her close. "Follow Hampstead. I'll stay here and see what Koslov does. And thanks for the dance." She grinned and patted her cheek.

"You are enjoying this far too much."

"Oh, yeah. Later."

Ellie left her at the bar in the room just off the dance floor and pushed to the second room, the lounge area. She took her phone out and pretended to check it as she scanned—ah. There was Marya holding court in a corner with her entourage and a bunch of other people she didn't recognize. One of them was taking photos as Marya posed with various members of her posse.

Still pretending to check her phone, Ellie instead snapped several photos of Marya's group, hoping they'd come out in this light. She was about to take another photo when someone walked past doused in cologne that smelled like Polo. Zaretsky? Ellie looked around casually but didn't see him right away. Before she let Rick and Sue know, she needed to make sure it was him and not some other dude who bought Polo in bulk and showered in it.

The cologne smell got stronger, and she looked around again. A guy walked right past her in a shiny black suit and yes, it was Zaretsky. She texted Rick and Sue and snapped a few photos of him as he worked his way through the crowd toward the room that separated the lounge from the dance floor.

She followed him, since Marya appeared to be doing fashion mogul things in the corner, and not involved in any arms trafficking at the moment. Zaretsky wasn't big like Koslov, so he was harder to spot, but when his cologne suddenly assailed her nostrils, she knew he was close. Someone should talk to him about that.

Finally, she got close enough to almost touch him as he kept moving toward the room with the dance floor. This was a man on a mission, from how he cleaved through the crowd. None of the casual side-stepping and smiles and nods that most people did in close quarters like this as they tried to maneuver. No, Zaretsky was clearly looking for someone, and it dawned on her that it might be Koslov.

Would he seriously try to pull something like shooting him on a dance floor? There would be witnesses to that, no matter how loud the music was. No time to text Sue as Zaretsky pushed onto the dance floor, and yes, he was working his way to Koslov, who was dancing happily in the center. Zaretsky's right hand went into his front pants pocket.

Not a gun. A knife, maybe? Ellie practically threw herself onto the floor and started dancing right in front of Zaretsky. He looked at her, annoyed, as she gave him an inviting smile. He pushed past her, but now he was forced to sort of move with the beat of the crowd, since it was like trying to swim against a strong current otherwise.

The music shifted and people slowed down. She used the moment to catch up with Zaretsky as he got even closer to Koslov, whose back was turned. Shit. Zaretsky was digging in his pocket again and sure enough, he pulled out what looked like a knife. Switchblade, most likely, since Zaretsky probably wouldn't want to risk stabbing other people with a loose blade on a packed dance floor.

She hooked one of her feet on Zaretsky's leg, and he stumbled a little, but the crowd kept him on his feet. He regained his balance, and she prepared to Flashdance herself right onto his back when Zaretsky stopped and jerked to his right. Someone had grabbed his wrist and as she watched, the guy managed to disarm him—how the hell? Zaretsky jerked his arm back, and the guy who had grabbed Zaretsky caught her eye and smiled before he was swallowed in the crowd, too.

It hit her, then, that the guy who had disarmed Zaretsky was Jonathan Hampstead. She dove into the crowd in the direction Zaretsky and Hampstead went. Zaretsky would most likely try to exit out the back, so she broke free of the dance floor and beelined for the door by the DJ booth.

"Ellie," Sue called.

A flash of white flitted at the edge of her peripheral vision. Sue, but she didn't have time to brief her. The door was just closing when Ellie got there, and she grabbed it and slipped through into the room beyond, which smelled of old beer, cigarettes, and Polo. She untucked her blouse and retrieved her gun.

A dim light overhead showed a narrow hallway, concrete floor, cheap paneling walls, and two doors on the right that were closed. Straight ahead, however, was another door, slowly closing. Ellie ran full-speed toward it and jerked it open to find ten or so steps that led to street level. The metal trapdoors were flung open. She scrabbled up the steps and hit her shin on one as she went to the sidewalk. A couple of people walked past, gave her a look, but continued on. No sign of Zaretsky or Daddy Hampstead— wait. Two guys running down the block, away from her.

She took off after them, ignoring the pain in her shin, glad she had flat-soled shoes because she was gaining on them. Zaretsky was in front, and Hampstead was a few steps behind him. Not bad for an older guy. She turned on another burst of speed and barreled between a couple of cars whose drivers honked and yelled at her.

In the streetlight a half-block up, Zaretsky threw himself into a dark panel van. Hampstead dropped into a shooter's pose, aiming at the van as it took off, tires squealing. Hampstead didn't fire. Instead, he straightened, shoved the gun into his pants, and stared after the van.

Ellie ducked into a doorway, panting. Hampstead might recognize her from the club. Please keep going, she silently pleaded with him. She returned her gun to its pocket and retucked her shirt. After a few beats, she took her jacket off and strolled out of the doorway, looking at her phone. She didn't hear anybody behind her, and she stopped.

Hampstead was gone, so she returned to the club and called Rick on the way.

"What the hell?" he said when he answered.

"Zaretsky just tried to stab Koslov on the dance floor."

"Jesus—"

"Jonathan Hampstead stopped him, and they both took off out the back. Zaretsky got into a dark van about three blocks from the bar, and Hampstead was armed. He didn't fire, but I had to take evasive measures. Lost him."

"Shit. What's your location?"

She jogged to the corner and gave him the streets.

"Can you get back into the club from the back?"

"I think so."

"Do it. Check on Marya. We'll canvass for Zaretsky and Jonathan."

"Got it." She hung up and put the phone back in her pocket. Her shin throbbed, and she carefully pulled her pants leg up. No bleeding, but it would have a nice bruise. She'd better wear trousers at work for the next few days.

"You okay?" Sue was waiting for her at the top of the steps at Lucky, looking like she was about to emerge from the underground.

"I'll live." She put her jacket back on.

"What happened?" Sue carefully backed down the steps to give her room.

Ellie gave her a brief rundown.

"Fucking hell."

"Yep. That sums it up." She closed the heavy steel interior door, making sure it clicked shut. At least nobody would be able to get in. Even back here, the thump of the dance music seemed to vibrate the walls. They were almost to the door that would take them back to the dance floor when one of the other doors in the hallway opened. Hell. Ellie didn't want to answer questions.

She grabbed Sue and pulled her into a kiss, much to Sue's shock, but she went with it, and her lips were soft and warm. A nice kiss, with a bit of heat, but it didn't move Ellie at all. Not even a little bit. No, apparently the only woman capable of making her feel anything from the waist down these days was an ice queen fashion mogul.

"Hey—" said a male voice.

Ellie pulled away and smiled at the guy, who she recognized as one of the bouncers from the front door. He had to be ex-military, and maybe fresh from that gig, because he still wore his hair like some of Rick's active Army buddies. "Hi," she said. "Sorry. Just getting some air." She gestured with her head at Sue, and the guy kind of smiled. Sue smiled at him, too.

"Can you blame me?" Sue said to him, hands on Ellie's shoulders.

"You're not supposed to be back here," he said, like he was trying to scold them, but maybe Ellie's charms and Sue's comment worked on him, because he was still smiling a little.

"Really sorry. Won't happen again." Ellie interlaced her fingers with Sue's and pulled her toward the dance floor.

The bouncer watched her, hands on his hips, and he practically filled the hallway, like the Hulk might. She pushed carefully through the door and pulled Sue inside.

"I'm going to check on Marya," she said near Sue's ear.

"Okay. I'll check the floor." She motioned at the dancers, and Ellie let go of her hand and worked her way back through the club to where she'd last seen Marya. And sure enough, Marya was still there with her posse and a whole bunch of new people.

She checked the time on her phone. Nearly one-thirty, and she was willing to bet that Marya would not be in the office tomorrow morning. She texted Rick and let him know that nothing had changed with Marya. A few seconds later he texted back that Koslov was still dancing, and it was time for her and Sue to pack it in. She texted an acknowledgement then let Sue know she'd meet her in the front room.

A few minutes later, Sue showed up, and they left together, Ellie with her arm around Sue's shoulders. "Where to?" she asked.

"Keep walking," she said. "Rick's sending a car to get us a couple of blocks up."

"Can the driver please bring pizza or something? I'm freaking starving." Ellie let go of her, and Sue immediately shoulder-bumped her.

"You got some mad lip skills too, O'Donnell." She gave her a sly grin.

"Sorry about that. Wasn't sure what else to do, given the circumstances."

"It worked. And damn, I have a whole new understanding of this lesbian thing."

"Yeah, well, I'm still not going to be your next field trip." She shoulder-bumped her back. "Though you are kind of hot. But I know I can't compete with Manny. His woman's safe from me."

She laughed, and they walked in silence for a few moments until she spoke again. "What the fuck with Zaretsky?"

"I don't know. First he's after Hampstead. Then Koslov. And why didn't he go after Hampstead? He was right there. Speaking of, when did Hampstead get to the club?" Ellie ran various scenarios through her head and nothing added up.

"Did Marya know her dad was in the house?"

Ellie stopped abruptly. Sue had taken a few paces beyond before she realized it.

"What?" Sue asked, waiting.

"That's a good question about Marya. I didn't see Jonathan on the dance floor. At least not near her. And he wasn't hanging out in fashion corner after she stopped dancing." She started walking again, still thinking.

"That's just fuckin' weird. Your dad's suddenly in town and he doesn't let you know?"

"And another question," Ellie said as they crossed a street. "How does an international businessman effectively disarm a Russian gangster like Zaretsky and then chase him out of a nightclub?" That was another weird aspect to this whole evening, and she thought back a couple of weeks ago, when she saw Daddy Hampstead checking reflections in the windows at the Fashion Forward building before she interrupted the Russians trailing him. Then he shows up at a nightclub and prevents, at the very least, a stabbing. At the most, a murder. Plus, he handled that gun like a boss.

Marya had seemed oblivious. And at last check, Daddy Hampstead was at a business expo in Chicago. Or at least, he'd left a trail to suggest such. Who the hell was this guy?

"Ride's here," Sue said as a sleek gray Town Car pulled to the curb.

"Since when did the department upgrade?" she asked as Sue opened the back door.

"Contract for when we have to do shit like this."

"You mean drive hot women around?"

"You complaining?"

"Only if there's no pizza."

Sue smacked her on the arm before she got in. Ellie waited for her to get settled, and then she got in and closed the door.

"Thanks," she said to the driver. "Any chance you could have a pizza waiting for me wherever we're going?"

"Not really my job description," the driver said as he pulled away from the curb.

"Figures." She texted Rick, asked for a pizza, then sat back and stared at the pale gray of the car's ceiling as Sue checked messages on her phone. What was she missing? What the hell was the deal with Jonathan Hampstead? And why would a Petrov associate suddenly want to stab Lyev Koslov? This was bad. Very bad.

She turned her head and stared out the window, still thinking, only now it was about Marya Hampstead on the dance floor, moving like foreplay, like she knew exactly what Ellie wanted and she would deliver it, but it would be so much hotter than she could even imagine.

A flush raced up her spine, which only got worse when she remembered how Marya had grabbed her and pulled her close and told her she liked her look. Was that flirting? Because it felt like it. Especially the grabbing part. Marya didn't have to do that. She didn't have to do or say anything like that to her. She could have just ignored Ellie the intern or just given her a polite smile and acknowledgement and that would've been that.

But she didn't.

And Ellie wondered what it would've felt like if Marya had kept pulling her close, until her lips made talking impossible. The flush spread all over her body and made a whole lot of things tingle, and made her think of other things. Like the fact that Marya liked a little bit of butch on a woman. And hold on, maybe a little bit of woman, too? That raised all kinds of interesting possibilities, since Marya had never been linked to women sexually. Not even in the gossip rags. If she had a thing for the ladies too, she kept it on hermetically sealed lockdown.

Another angle to think about, but not until she'd had something to eat, followed by some sleep. She closed her eyes and let herself appreciate the quiet of the car, and please, for the love of God, she hoped Rick had a pizza waiting for her.

CHAPTER 8

"So nobody saw Daddy Hampstead go into the club?" Ellie asked, but it sounded more like "So body raw Ded Hamp go inna club" because she was chewing on a huge bite of pizza.

"That's disgusting. Didn't your mama tell you not to talk with your mouth full?" Rick gave her a long-suffering stare.

She swallowed. "Whatever. Answer the question."

"We're going back through security footage. Did he have a hat on or anything?"

She thought for a bit. "No. Dark shirt. Dark pants. But he could have had one on when he went in." She finished her third piece of pizza and reached for another.

Rick stared at her fourth slice, wide-eyed.

"What? I told you I was hungry."

"What about a salad every now and then?"

"Not tonight." She took a bite. "Mmm. So good." She chewed for a bit and swallowed. "Something's not right about Hampstead."

"No shit." Rick glanced over at Wes, the other guy running recon on this shift. "Anything?" Rick asked him.

"Nada, bro. I've got a couple of other people on it, too, running the surveillance videos super-slow, to see if we can pick him out."

"Dude, seriously," Ellie said. "Hampstead isn't just a businessman. The guy knew he was being tailed two weeks ago when I blendered Laskin's knee, and he disarmed Zaretsky, no big deal, on a crowded dance floor. And you should've seen his stance when he pulled the gun after Zaretsky got into the van. He's got to have training in that sort of thing. But there's no record of military service in his background."

"Black ops," Wes said, his gaze locked onto the computer screen. "If he was doing that shit, it wouldn't show up in his record."

"But if he had any military experience, that should show up, right?" She looked at Rick. "I mean, there would be a record of military service, and it would be all benign if he was black opping."

"Maybe," Rick said. He frowned. "I've got a military buddy in London. I'll ask him if they do that over there."

She finished the piece of pizza and washed it down with bottled water, her concession tonight to Rick's plea for her to eat better. "So let's pretend he's got some kind of training. He retires from the military and goes into business, but he knows all kinds of people from his military days. The kinds of people in illegal arms. So he does that on the side. If he's responsible for taking out those Petrov guys overseas, maybe he did them himself."

Rick grunted and took a swig of water from his own bottle. "What about Marya and Lyev? Just hanging out?"

"Yep. Looked like a celebrity night out, basically. And then she hung out in a corner with a bunch of worshippers while Koslov was dancing his ass off."

"He could've passed her something," Rick said. "A note. A wad of cash. A flash drive."

"Well, he picked a good place to do it." She leaned back in her chair and put her feet on her desk. It was almost three in the damn morning, and here she was at the office.

"Boys and girls, we have a winner. Check this out."

She groaned as she got up with Rick. She'd just gotten comfortable.

"See this?" Wes pointed at the screen, and Rick and Ellie leaned in. "Daddy Hampstead. Black shirt, black pants, black fedora."

"Classy. Kind of a Michael Jackson thing. Does he have a glove on?" Ellie leaned close, and Rick snorted. She looked at the timestamp. A little after twelve-thirty.

"So he goes in and—" he clicked on some stuff, and another angle from the club popped up, this one in the front room. "Checks his hat and then here he is, hanging out by the bar. And ten minutes later, Zaretsky arrives."

She watched as Zaretsky scanned the room. Daddy Hampstead had insinuated himself into a conversation with a couple of women and a guy, but as soon as Zaretsky moved into the lounge room, Hampstead waited a beat then followed.

"This guy *is* good," Rick said. "Bet he didn't know those people he was just talking to."

Wes switched the video to the lounge room. Zaretsky looked around there, but took his time. Hampstead entered and immediately started talking to a woman who looked like she was on her way to the bar. Whatever he said, it made her laugh. He ignored Marya, who probably didn't even see him. Zaretsky then went into the next room.

"Here's where you pick up on him, E," Wes said. "Check it."

"Damn, my hair looks good."

Rick snorted again.

He slowed the video down even more. "Zaretsky walks past you and goes into the dance floor room. You go after him. Meanwhile, Jonathan Hampstead is here." He pointed at Hampstead, who was standing near the second bar. "And now to the dance floor."

"There's Koslov," Rick said. "And here comes Zaretsky."

"O'Donnell with the sexy dance interruption." Wes chortled.

"Let me see that again," Rick said.

He ran it back, and Rick laughed. "Good move, Els. But Zaretsky's not having it and—"

"Boom! O'Donnell with the foot check!" Wes doubled over laughing.

"Shut up." She smacked him lightly on the back of the head.

"Good play, Els. Opened a lane for Hampstead. But the camera didn't pick up the disarm. Too many freakin' people blocking the view."

"Trust me. It was smooth."

"Not as smooth as the dance interruption." Wes grinned at her. "Okay, Koslov makes a run for it out the back, with Hampstead on his ass. Shitty lighting for the camera in the back hallway, but you can kind of see—" he called up the video from that camera, and he was right. You could kind of see a couple of shapes moving quickly, then a bit more light as Zaretsky threw the back door open.

"Unfortunately, no camera near that entrance. Club owner says it broke a couple nights ago, and it won't be replaced until Monday. So we don't really know what happened, except the two of them got out. And now here comes O'Donnell," he said. "Nice run."

Ellie watched herself barrel down the hallway, and then she couldn't see anything else. A few seconds later, a blur of white entered the screen. That was Sue, also running. Wes shut the video off, much to Ellie's relief. They hadn't seen her grab Sue and kiss her back there, and hopefully they never would. The things she did for national security.

"Got any good leads from the Hampstead cell phones?" she asked.

"Nope," Wes said. "Unless they're speaking in really excellent code. We're going back through those, too. But if Daddy Hampstead was black ops, they're probably using burn phones."

"Marya has a flip phone, remember," Ellie said. "But maybe she's having illicit affairs all over the place, and that's why she uses a burn phone. Hell, it's easy these days to tap a phone. Have you seen what the paparazzi do?"

"Or maybe dear Dad has sucked her into his arms business, and they're using Fashion Forward as a front," Rick said.

"I'm not sold on that yet. Daddy might be, but maybe he doesn't tell Daughter what he's up to. He didn't even stop to chat in the club. So he gives her a burn phone and tells her to call him on that, because he doesn't want business competition to know what he's up to. Maybe he's just weird and has a paranoid streak, and Marya's been dealing with it her whole life, so she humors him."

Rick shook his head, skeptical.

"Or," she continued, "because Dad was black ops, she knows he has to be careful with some shit, and she's okay with the burn phone as part of life as she knows it. It could be anything, and so far, the only thing we've got is she hangs out sometimes with Lyev Koslov and there's a Koslov model in her stable. Which could be totally benign. Maybe Lyev asked Marya if she'd have a look at Natalie's portfolio and that's how there's a Koslov on the roster."

"Your point?" Rick asked.

"I've been there two freaking weeks and you've been monitoring her longer, and we still have *nothing* to prove there's shit going on at Fashion Forward. And it's three-thirty in the goddamn morning and I'm fucking tired. That's my point." And it was. Her bones practically ached she was so exhausted.

Rick's expression softened. "You're right. Can you crash here?"

"I kind of have to or I won't get any damn sleep, since it's at least thirty minutes driving to the apartment. I've got some outfits here, don't worry. Seriously. I'm going to crash, and Rick knows my cranky side is not pretty."

"I can tell. Thanks for your help." Wes waved, and Ellie went to the room just off the station locker room that had a couple of cots set up for occasions such as this. She took her shoes off and stretched out. She was too tired to even undress. The last thought on her mind was why the hell she was trying so hard to defend Marya Hampstead.

Considering she felt like the ass-end of a long weekend in Tijuana, Ellie looked okay. She checked her face in the mirror. No dark circles under her eyes, though she did look a little tired. Because of the huge bruise on her shin, she'd worn trousers today. Black slim line, with tapered ankles because fuck it, it was Friday and definitely a wingtip day. Her blouse was a tad on the feminine side, but she liked its classic lines and French cuffs. Off-white with muted red pinstripes. She'd left the top two buttons undone, and a simple silver chain decorated her neck, which matched the simple silver cufflinks she wore. By the end of this assignment, she'd be shopping using proper clothing terminology.

It was also definitely time for another cup of coffee.

Her work phone dinged with a text message. Rick, telling her to call ASAP. He wouldn't ask that of her while she was here unless it was urgent. She left Fashion Forward and took the elevator down to street level. Once outside, she dialed Rick's number

"Hey," she said. "What's up?"

"Zaretsky turned up dead."

"Shit. Where?"

"Pier near the Washington Bridge. Gunshot to the head. Execution style."

"Like the other three?"

"Looks that way."

Ellie thought immediately of Jonathan Hampstead. "We're sure it's Zaretsky?"

"Pretty sure. Some distinguishing gangster tattoos. We got a local LEO courtesy call. We're trying to get jurisdiction over the body."

"Found the body quick. What's that about?"

"Tip called in."

Ellie frowned. "Why the hell would you kill a dude then phone it in? 'Oh, hey, sorry about the mess, but I left a body.'"

"We're digging. If I didn't know better, there's a public relations element going on here." Rick paused and said something to somebody else, then he was back. "Koslov might be warning Petrov."

Ellie put a candy in her mouth. "Huh. We know about your boy, here, and this is what happens if you try to do shit like this while we're in secret talks about murders overseas? Like that?"

"That's about right. Otherwise, why call in a tip?"

The cinnamon burned her tongue. "Any sign of Daddy Hampstead?"

"Nope. Dude's in the wind. Hell, he might *be* the wind. Everybody at his bank says he's in Chicago."

"Well, aren't they all well-trained? Any idea when Zaretsky died?"

"Estimate is around four this morning, based on your timeline."

She'd last seen him around two. She ran a hand through her hair, frustrated and still tired. She started walking toward the corner. Across the street was a Starbucks. "Maybe whoever was in the van shot him."

"Seems likely. Doesn't sound like Hampstead was in on this one, unless he knows that van and was able to track it down. We might know more after they're done processing the scene." He didn't sound convinced, and given where the body was found, Ellie doubted they'd find much of anything. They needed that van if they were going to follow this part of the case.

"You gonna talk to the Petrovs?" Ellie paused at the street and waited for the light.

"Already on it. I've got a call into Daddy Petrov. And yes, I'll talk to the Koslovs, too."

"What about my model search? Anything on Natalie Koslov?"

"Like Liz said, she's a niece of Daddy Koslov. Daughter of his oldest sister. We're still running more down. Watch your six, Els." He hung up, and Ellie crossed the street, thinking, but nothing was making sense.

What if Jonathan Hampstead wasn't a businessman and wasn't an arms dealer? What if he was doing black ops for some government agency somewhere? But if he was, then why would he kill all those Petrovs? And Zaretsky? That seemed like a waste of good information right there. Unless he *didn't* kill them.

If he was some kind of government spook, maybe he was trying to find out who was killing Petrovs, and he got really close, which was why he was in the same cities as the guys who died. He got that close, but not close enough.

And this sounded totally insane, like a damn *Bourne* movie.

The smell of strong coffee welcomed her as she went into Starbucks and got in line. Fortified with a giant cup, she went back to Fashion Forward, cradling her coffee like it was the last on the planet. When she arrived in the lobby of Fashion Forward, Tyler cornered her in front of the reception desk.

"Thanks for the layouts. Do you have some time now to go over tomorrow again?"

Tomorrow. Ellie stared at him. Oh, yeah. The fashion show. Hell. Please let her get some sleep tonight. "Yes. How about now?"

"Super."

She followed him to his office and listened as he gave her the rundown. "Questions?" he asked about fifteen minutes later.

"I don't think so."

"Well, you've got my cell phone, and we'll all be in contact via headset if anything goes sideways."

"Like what?" It was a fashion show, not a military op.

"Model meltdown. Some of them are precious," he said wryly, and Ellie almost spit her coffee out.

Tyler's eyes practically twinkled. "Marya would agree."

She looked at him. He called her Marya? They were tighter than she'd thought.

"So they might flip out over having the wrong kind of bottled water or something?"

He laughed. "One never knows. See you tomorrow morning."

She got up and went back to her office. Liz was out today, which was a relief. As nice as she was, Ellie was not in the mood to deal with a side of extra perky. Instead, she opened her personal laptop and went to the events page on Natalie Koslov's website. She took a screenshot of it before she went through more carefully. All the usual fashion sites. Milan, Paris, London, and yes, Moscow.

Sure, Moscow was on the international fashion circuit. But what interesting things that brought up here.

Natalie Koslov, an American-born model who just happened to be a niece of a high-powered Russian dude who owned a company in Moscow. Shipments from that company were actually discovered to be illegal arms. So if you're not running guns domestically up the I-95 corridor—practically the supermarket of gunrunning from the south to NYC—you're needing to touch base with international contacts. They need to get their orders to you. Some they might be able to send via email, through a front on a website. But in this world of high-tech surveillance, how do you stay on the down-low with that?

Burn phones and maybe some old-school face-to-face. Daddy Koslov didn't travel if he didn't have to, and he hadn't been out of the country for over a year.

But Natalie had been. She traveled all the time, to major cities all over Europe and at least one major city in Russia. Ellie stared at the website. What if Natalie was a point of contact? People could put their orders in with her, and she'd hook Daddy Koslov up with them. She was his niece, after all. It wouldn't be weird for her to do that. And maybe they had some kind of code. Or she could just funnel the info to someone else who would then forward it to Daddy Koslov.

Someone who was tuned into the celebrity scene, who hung out with models and moguls all the time.

Or someone who *was* those things.

Lyev Koslov could be working alone with Natalie, or Marya was in on it, too.

She groaned. The other option was that she was running on too little sleep and these ruminations were the product of exhaustion and stress. Her e-chat dinged with a pop-up indicating a message from Tyler: *Drinks after work with some of the staff?*

Oh, God. Really? Another night out? Did fashion mogul staff never sleep? She took another swallow of coffee and messaged him back: *Sure. Where and when?* "Please let it be right after work," she muttered.

The answer came quickly. *Five-thirty, Pig and Pint, two blocks up Fifth.*

She knew the place. A pub that showed a lot of soccer on TVs hung over the bar. Casual, and it offered booths that were semi-private. Probably a good place for fashion mogul types to unwind, out of sight of the dragon lady. Have a few beers, nachos or wings, and commiserate about the high pressure involved in selling ridiculously expensive and often weird-ass clothing to the masses even though it only looked good on women shaped like clothespins. And thank all the deities who had heard her plea about the time. She might be able to get home at a reasonable hour for some sleep, because making sure models had their proper bottled water was something everyone should aspire to on a Saturday morning.

CHAPTER 9

Ellie finished the tasks Tyler had assigned and moved onto checking videos of Natalie Koslov's most recent appearances on catwalks, including her Moscow trip the previous month. Those links Ellie sent to Rick with a message telling him to have the team look through the audiences, see if anybody pinged their arms-dealer radars. If Natalie was the point of contact for her Uncle Koslov, then there was a possibility that some of the customers attended her shows.

The Petrovs had to fit in here somewhere, too. Ellie did a few more standard web searches using the names of the dead men and got several hits. Clearly, they weren't shy about using their names, and *hello*, they were in attendance at three specific fashion shows. Moscow a week before the first murder, Prague three days before the second, and London the night before the third death.

What the hell did this mean? Ellie ate another cinnamon candy and called Rick.

"What's up?" he answered.

"Dude, did anyone check our dead guys' connections to fashion shows other than me?"

Silence.

"So that's a no. Well, I got something. Shows in each of the cities a few days before each of them died. Run that shit. Get lists of guests, if possible, and the models involved. And I want a raise."

He laughed. "I'll see what I can do. Nice find."

"Damn right. I'm also going out for drinks with Jackson and some other staff, but he didn't say who. Pig and Pint on Fifth. Five-thirty."

"Okay. You hereby have official permission to imbibe a couple for the sake of appearances. Check in after."

"Yep." She hung up and stared at the clock on her laptop. An hour to go. So how about she dug around on the Petrovs some more? See what else she could turn up. Thirty minutes later, she hadn't turned anything up that she didn't already know, so she tried a web search on models with the last name of Petrov.

"Well, lookee here."

Yana Petrov, based in London. She called Rick back.

"People are going to start rumors about us if you keep calling this much," he said when he picked up.

"Whatever. Yana Petrov. Found her on the model circuit. Run her and see how she relates to Daddy Petrov, if at all. While you're at it, see how many Petrovs and Koslovs are modeling."

"Aren't you just full of helpful tips."

"See to that raise, bro." She hung up. Yana had a website, so Ellie spent some time on it. Yana had been born in St. Petersburg, Russia, but worked primarily in London. Her events schedule, however, had her all over Europe and the US, like Natalie Koslov. On another hunch, Ellie did a search on both names to see if they'd pop up in any context together.

Yes. At two shows the year before and, most recently, in Paris and Moscow. Was Petrov scheduled for tomorrow's show? Ellie popped back over to Petrov's website but didn't find it listed in the events. The next thing Petrov had coming up was in Los Angeles in a month.

There might be something here, she thought. Or there might be nothing at all. She shut her laptop down and put it in her bag along with her work and personal phones, then finished the last of the coffee and tossed the cup in the trash. It was quarter after five, but it would take her a few minutes to get to the pub, so she put her jacket on— the same one she'd worn the night before—and slung her bag over her shoulder.

The fashion world apparently never slept and never stopped, because people were still bustling around in the lobby, on their way to offices or getting more coffee. Ellie waved to the receptionist and made the elevator just as it was closing, which earned her an irritated glare from an older guy in the back. She ignored him and shoved herself in. A couple of people chatted about some kind of real estate thing on the way down, and a few others were messing with their phones.

They finally arrived at the ground floor and Ellie stepped off the elevator with relief. She wasn't a fan of close quarters like that, especially when there was nowhere to go. The weather had stayed nice, though a bit cool. Fall was her favorite season in the city. September was a transitional sort of month, and it always carried hints of impending autumn in the breezes and drop in humidity. And with the nice evening weather, there would be lots of people out, enjoying it and the end of the work week for many of them.

Ellie didn't often get a Friday off, because her job had her on different schedules every month. Plus, given the nature of the work she did for this division of NYPD, it seemed she was always on call. Then again, cops were always on call, regardless, even when they weren't. Rick had been after her to take a vacation since she hadn't in a couple of years, but she liked her job too much. Her parents had thought she was insane when she pursued police work. Since they were both teachers, they had no idea where she'd gotten that urge. Too much adrenaline in the womb, her sister used to tease her.

Anymore, Ellie wondered if there was something to that.

The Pig and Pint was just ahead, its front evoking what an Irish pub might look like if it were actually in Ireland. Glossy green paint around the front windows and door trim made the place look festive, and the name was painted in gold across the glass. She went in, and it smelled like most other bars, minus the cigarette smoke. Beer, bar food, and various colognes. It was about halfway full. Tyler waved at her from a booth, which was a high-backed wooden affair that looked more like an alcove. Each side of the table could seat three.

"Hey," he said as she approached. Khalil and Liz sat on his side.

"Hi," she said, and Tyler motioned at the empty side. She sat down and put her bag and jacket next to her.

"We just ordered a few minutes ago," Tyler said. "Drinks and snacks."

"Sounds good. I'll throw in for snacks." She smiled, trying to be her suave, professional self.

"So how are things going for you, as Ms. H's intern?" Liz asked.

"Pretty well. I feel like I'm learning a lot and all of you have been really helpful and nice."

"Really? I thought you had met Ms. H," Liz said with a smile.

"Oh, she has," Khalil said. "And she's lived to talk about it. As for me, I'm currently on her good side."

Tyler laughed. "Marya liked one of Ellie's ideas."

Liz's eyes widened. "You didn't tell me that."

"Beginner's luck," Ellie said.

The server appeared with a tray of drinks. Khalil had ordered what looked like a gin and tonic, Liz a martini, and Tyler's was most likely a vodka cranberry.

"Hi," the server said to Ellie, all bippy with an understated Irish lilt. "What'll you have?"

"Do you have Red Breast?"

The server brightened even more. "Yes."

"I'll take one of those, neat."

The server smiled. "Excellent. Would you like to order any food?"

"I think we're covered for now." She looked at Tyler, and he nodded.

"Great. Just let me know if you change your mind." She gave Ellie another smile and retreated to the bar.

"We should bring you here more often," Khalil said. "She rarely gives me the time of day."

Liz giggled. "You're not her type."

"And we will use it to our advantage," Tyler said. "Anyway, Khalil and a few others you know will be on hand tomorrow as well."

"Thank God. Now if there's a meltdown over the bottled water, I'll have backup."

Liz giggled again and carefully sipped her drink.

"Where will you be?" Ellie asked her.

"I'll be watching from the audience."

"Nice. One of the chosen." She looked up as the server returned with her glass of whiskey.

"Here you go. Let me know if you need anything else."

Khalil smirked, but Ellie pretended not to see it.

"Your food will be right out." She retreated again, but not before she gave Ellie another cute little smile. That was definitely flirting, Ellie decided. This haircut worked with more than just being an intern at a fashion mag.

"I think she likes you," Tyler teased.

She shrugged and took a sip of the whiskey. Smooth and warm, it flowed down her throat like velvet. A good ending to this day.

The server was back a few seconds later with a plate of hot wings, cheese fries, and a cheese and veggie platter. So the crew liked bar food. Ellie approved. It made them more down-to-earth. "Flag me down for anything else," the server said.

"Thanks." Ellie smiled at her, and Khalil gave her a surreptitious thumbs-up.

"Khalil has worked a few other shows," Tyler said, "and he can give you some pointers."

"Great. Walk me through what I need to do the minute I get there." She took one of the appetizer plates and loaded it up with fries and cheese and veggies. She might go for a wing later, but given the color of her shirt, she didn't want to risk a food accident, though Khalil would totally sympathize. Maybe he even had an extra shirt with him.

Khalil described a typical first couple of hours backstage at a show, with Tyler adding a few things. Liz told her to try to get out front so she could watch some of the walks, which were pretty cool, apparently.

"This all sounds intense," Ellie said, "but I'm sure I'll learn a lot. I really appreciate you all taking the time to help me." She pushed the cheese fry platter toward Khalil, who seemed to be as into them as she was. He enthusiastically served himself another helping and pushed the plate back to her.

She started to serve herself some more when a well-modulated British accent said, "Hello, everyone. Happy Friday."

"Hi, Ms. H," Khalil and Liz said on one accord.

Ellie grabbed a napkin and started to stand, trying to cover her shock at Marya joining the peons and addressing them in such a casual way. And oh, Lord, she was wearing a black Forties-style skirt and an off-white silk blouse that moved with her like a second skin. Simple, but on Marya, it looked like a million dollars.

"Don't worry about it," Marya said. "Just slide over." And she smiled. Holy Christ on a surfboard, Marya Hampstead busted out a full smile, and it washed over Ellie like a warm, delicious wave. It lit her eyes up with sparks and promises and made Ellie think of last night on the dance floor, when Marya's lips had been really close to her ear.

"Sure," Ellie said, sounding smooth, though fireworks were shooting up and down her legs. She scooched over, pushing her bag and jacket along the wooden seat of the bench until both were against the wall. She also left room between her and Marya, because the dragon lady's hotness was dangerous. It was at that moment that she noticed one of Marya's security dudes sitting at a table near the booth, checking his phone. Ellie wondered if Daddy Hampstead had checked in with her, or if Marya even knew he was in town.

"Hi, Marya." The server seemed to have teleported from the kitchen or something, because she was suddenly next to the table. "The usual?"

Marya settled herself next to Ellie. "Yes, thanks."

She shifted her gaze to Ellie. "Another?"

"Yes." She smiled at her. "Appreciate it." And hello, but Marya was a regular here? She actually went out with staff on a regular basis?

"Anybody else?" the server asked.

The other three ordered another round, and Tyler added another cheese and veggie platter.

The server bounced to the security dude's table, got his order, and then went to the bar. Ellie picked up her glass. She still had a bit of whiskey, and oh, she needed it.

For her part, Marya talked to Khalil and then Tyler. Liz looked anxious and kept toying with her empty glass. Marya asked her about a project she was working on, and Liz answered with a nervous lilt to her voice. Ellie watched Marya out of her peripheral vision, pretending to care what everybody else was up to. So out of the office, she was less dragon, more lady? Which jibed with what Gwen had told her.

The server reappeared with drinks and set a tall glass garnished with strawberry, cucumber, apple, and a sprig of mint in front of Marya. She placed the other drinks in front of their respective owners and left again.

"Pimm's cup," Marya said, and Ellie realized she'd been busted scoping out Marya's glass. And her fingers, which were manicured, but she was not wearing colored nail polish today. "They make a very good one here," Marya added. "Authentic." She gestured at Ellie's glass. "Which whiskey?"

"Red Breast."

The hint of another smile danced at the corner of her mouth, and all of Ellie's internal organs felt like they were doing gymnastics.

"Excellent choice," she said.

Liz's eyes widened at this approval from the ice queen.

"And how are you finding Fashion Forward, Ms. Daniels?" Marya asked as she stirred her drink.

"Fast-paced, informative, busy, sometimes intense. And I've decided I kind of like the coffee."

Liz stared at her. Ellie caught her gaze and gave her a tiny shrug. She hid her smile behind the rim of her glass.

Tyler laughed, and Marya smiled as she sipped her drink. Oh, how Ellie wanted to be the glass—whoa, hold up. Get a grip. You may have to arrest this woman.

But holy hell, Marya was doing all kinds of crazy things to her nerves.

And other parts of her body.

Without even trying.

Fortunately, Marya directed the conversation to other projects at the mag, and Ellie relaxed a bit. She could listen to her talk all day in that voice and accent. Even if it was just reciting grocery lists, which made her feel like a provincial American, but so what? That accent wrapped in the package that was Marya Hampstead? Who wouldn't want to hear that all day?

"We're trying your Agent Carter suggestion," Marya said, and Ellie snapped immediately to attention.

"It looks...well, excellent." Tyler grinned at her. "You'll see the layouts next week."

"Glad I could help."

Liz stared at Ellie again, while Khalil was busy with the remains of the fries. Fortunately for him, the server appeared with the second cheese and veggie platter along with a clean stack of appetizer plates.

"Everybody good?" she asked and, at the affirmatives, moved efficiently away with the dirties to check on other tables. There were only three servers, and this place was getting pretty busy.

Marya placed several pieces of cheese on her plate along with a bunch of carrots and cucumbers. And olives. That was heartening. Olives were important in Ellie's world. Not that it mattered. There was zero chance of anything between her and Hampstead. Fun to think about, though.

"How do you envision the Agent Carter theme playing out?" she asked Marya.

"Very well. It's classic, like you said, but also playful. And maybe a little dangerous. I made it a point to watch the first season of the show, which made me like your suggestion even more."

Ellie reached for her glass. "Have you watched the second season?"

"Just started it."

"I love Agent Carter," Tyler admitted. "Down-to-earth glamour."

Marya stared at him. "That. Write that down."

"Got it," Khalil said, holding his phone up.

"We can use that." Marya took a bite of cheese, and Ellie melted inside. The ice queen was human and had to eat actual food. "I have to say, Ms. Daniels," she continued, "I haven't had the best luck with interns prior to you."

Liz's eyes were practically popping out of her head.

She took another sip of whiskey to distract herself from the throbbing between her legs. "Call me Ellie. And I'm just grateful for the chance to contribute. Who knew my Agent Carter habit could prove useful?"

Khalil popped a piece of cheese into his mouth. "I'm halfway through the first season. I'm kind of loving it."

"That's another one of my secret alternative career choices." Ellie bit into a carrot.

"Secret agent?" Tyler asked.

"Well, that. And writer for a TV show like that. I think that might be easier than the secret agent part."

At that moment, Marya's leg brushed hers. When did Marya get close enough to do that? Or had Ellie done it? Shit. She shifted a little to her left. Not enough to be obvious, but enough so that she wouldn't be in contact with Marya's leg. Which was most distracting. Though incredibly arousing.

"Secret agent," Marya said, and it sounded thoughtful, as if she was considering the idea. "Any particular reason why?"

"Not really," she said, enjoying the irony in this conversation. "It looks like fun. And interesting."

"And dangerous," Khalil said.

"I think Ellie could probably handle it." Tyler stirred his drink before he took a sip.

"Indeed," Marya said, and then somebody's cell phone rang with the sound reserved for old-school rotary dials. Marya dug her phone out of her bag and glanced at it. "I have to take this." She got up and went over to her security guard's table.

Liz tapped Tyler's shoulder, and he slid out of the booth so she could get out. Ellie guessed she was on her way to the restroom. When Liz was out of earshot, Tyler leaned forward, conspiratorial.

"You are privy to a major secret," he said with a little smirk.

"That Marya Hampstead has been binge-watching Agent Carter? I'll take it to my grave."

Khalil giggled, and Tyler's smirk turned into a smile. "That's part of the secret. But as you no doubt have started to realize, Marya cultivates a certain public persona, and she does it very well."

"You mean the ice queen thing?"

Tyler sipped his drink. "That's one of the milder terms for it. And yes."

"Why?"

"It gives her an edge in this industry, and it ensures that her private life stays private. If you have a rep like that, and it involves going after paparazzi, for example, and shutting inquiries down, people tend to leave you alone, or they're more respectful about how they approach you."

Which meant that Marya was a rare celebrity who actually retained a lot of control over her image. "So what makes me special, to be in on this?" She picked up a piece of cheese and glanced over at Marya, who was still on the phone and from her body language, she was back in ice queen mode. She looked back at Tyler.

"Marya is a very good judge of character," he said, and she suddenly felt guilty, because she was totally not at all what Marya thought. It sucked, sometimes, that she was so good at lying. And it bugged her that she was lying to Marya about everything.

"I'm flattered," she said.

"You should be." Tyler munched on a cucumber slice, and Marya returned.

"That was Reggie. He'll be calling you to finish with some details." She sat back down and sure enough, his phone rang.

"No rest for the wicked," Ellie said as he got up and went to the security guard's table. She liked all this politeness in the modern world.

Khalil slid out of the booth, too. "Be right back," he said and moved toward the entrance. Probably wanted to smoke. And oh, hell, here she was, sitting next to Marya Hampstead. Inches between them.

"Do you go to Lucky often?" Marya asked. Her gaze pinned Ellie's, and she almost forgot what language she spoke.

"I haven't been in a while," she said, applauding herself because she didn't sound completely idiotic. "A friend of mine has been after me for a while to get out a bit more. Something about working too hard. Not that you'd know anything about that." She picked up her glass with a little smile and sipped. Careful with the liquid courage, she warned herself.

"Not at all," Marya said, teasing right back.

"I figured. Running a fashion empire is clearly a piece of cake." She sipped again. "A very complicated, multilayer, extremely pretty, and well-attuned cake, but cake nonetheless." Oh, shit. Too much liquid courage.

But good God, Marya Hampstead laughed. Actually laughed. And it sounded like the way excellent whiskey tasted. Rich and tangy on the front end but warm and soft on the back. There was far too much sexy in that laugh. Fuck.

"On another note, I notice things," Marya said.

Ellie had figured that out right away. She waited for her to continue.

Marya ran her fingertip over the rim of her glass. "And one of the things I noticed about you is that you're not easily intimidated."

She kept her mouth shut. This was Marya Hampstead, after all. She could whip out the dragon lady any time and kill mere mortals with a glare.

"I appreciate that, because it's hard to find people I can rely on in this business. Many lose their perspective."

"Starstruck?" she asked. Her glass was her new best friend, because it kept her hand busy and made sure she wasn't nervously tapping her fingers on the table.

"Frankly, yes."

She realized that Marya, though the type of woman who commanded respect, was also interested in people who looked past the persona. It made her human, maybe a little vulnerable, and she felt even worse about the dossier she'd pored over and all the information she'd accumulated on her. It made her feel creepy and sort of stalker-ish. Especially sitting here with her, enjoying a drink. And her smile. And laugh.

And it was seriously time to go, before shit got out of hand. Fortunately, Tyler returned.

"Done," he said. "And it's about time for dinner."

Marya glanced at her phone and a little frown creased her forehead. Ellie wanted to stroke it smooth. Or kiss it.

Seriously. It was time to go.

"I suppose so." Marya didn't sound enthused, and Ellie looked at Tyler.

"We have a dinner date with a few of the designers who will be showing tomorrow." He shrugged and finished the last piece of cheese from the now sad, picked-over platter. Khalil appeared, Liz with him. Maybe she'd been out smoking with him.

"Good to see you outside of work," he said to Ellie.

"Yes. I certainly enjoyed talking about work outside of work," she said with a grin as she finished the last of her whiskey.

Tyler laughed, and Liz kept glancing from him to Marya, as if she was trying to figure out what cue to take.

"Well," Marya said. "I'm sorry to cut this short. But I'll see you tomorrow." She got up, and Ellie was both relieved and disappointed.

"Definitely." She looked at Tyler. "What do I owe you for my share?"

"Don't worry about it."

"Are you sure?"

"Yes. Taken care of. See you tomorrow.

She grabbed her jacket and bag and slid out of the booth. "All right. Thanks again. See everybody tomorrow." She put her jacket on just as the server appeared.

"Thanks, everyone," she said. "And thanks, Marya. Good to see you."

"And you. Please send your parents my best."

"I will. 'Til next time," she said to Tyler and Khalil, who gave her brief hugs and made their way to the door, Liz trailing after.

"I hope to see you again, too," the server said to Ellie. She raised her eyebrows playfully.

"Sounds good. Looking forward to it."

The server smiled and set to work clearing the table because people were already standing around waiting for it. Ellie turned to go and realized that Marya was standing with her security guard, and she had a quizzical little smile tugging at the corners of her perfect mouth.

"You passed her test," Marya said.

"I don't even know what it was." She adjusted her bag and followed Marya and the guard through the knots of people toward the front door.

"She appreciates women who drink good whiskey." And then they were outside, and she turned and faced Ellie. "As do I."

And Ellie fell right into the warm depths of her eyes, right into this other Marya—the one with the teasing sense of humor and the amazing laugh and the smiles that lit up entire city blocks. That was the Marya Hampstead she saw tonight, and God help her, she wanted to see much, much more.

"Have a good night," Marya said. "See you tomorrow."

"Yep. You will. Good night." She smiled, waved, and walked away before she got herself into any more trouble. Definitely needed to walk a bit, get some perspective, because this might be more dangerous than an arms-dealing ring. This was a serious attraction, the kind that kept you up at night and left you burning all day. This was a once-in-a-very-long-while kind of attraction and it came at the absolute worst time, in the worst possible circumstances.

Get to work, she reminded herself. She called Rick.

"Hey," he answered.

"I'm assuming you have somebody on Marya. She's having dinner with Jackson for sure, as well as some fashion designers. Don't know where, but they're on their way."

"We are on it. Did you know she was going to show up tonight?"

"Hell, no. Shock city. But convenient for us."

"She seems to be warming up to you. What was the topic of discussion?"

"You're kidding, right?" She dodged a group of people laughing and talking. "What else do fashion moguls talk about with their staff? The upcoming fashion show tomorrow. And I am going to go home and get some sleep so I can be on point with that. I'll call you when I get there, because I have a hunch."

"Uh-oh. An O'Donnell hunch."

"Yeah, whatever. They're usually pretty good."

"This is true. You do have about a seventy-two percent success rate with hunches."

"You're funny, Rick. This is me laughing." She hung up and went down the stairs to the subway, working very hard to keep images of Marya out of her head and pretty much failing all the way to the sterile apartment in Brooklyn.

CHAPTER 10

So this was fashion on display. Ellie watched the models work the runway, timing their motions, poses, and spins to the music, staring out at the crowd. It was sort of like performance art, only everybody took it seriously. Natalie Koslov strutted onto the runway, and she had some kind of indefinable charisma that drew gazes right away. Models probably needed that to get noticed by the fashion houses.

It wasn't just about Koslov's physical appearance, which was angular, thin, and willowy, as expected of fashion culture—no, she had an underlying something that she threw around on the runway, and it exhibited as sly little smiles and cocky little head and hip jerks. Not like most of the other models, who maintained bland, affectless demeanors so as to make people focus on the clothing.

Natalie Koslov made you look at *her* as well the clothing, made you think about the woman beneath the clothes. Of everyone here, she might be the one person up there who really was engaging in performance art.

Ellie headed backstage to check in with Khalil preemptively, before she got some frantic message over her headset. Plus, the more time she spent around the models, the better the chances of seeing something out of place, based on her theory. She'd already taken video of the audience and sent it to Rick.

She'd worn slim tapered trousers in a metallic gray that she had to admit looked really good with her black wingtips. The fashion consultant had told her that metallic colors worked well on blondes as did white, so Ellie's shirt was that color, though the wide 40s-style tie she wore was dark blue with slashes of bright yellow. She also wore a light gray blazer tailored to give Ellie more room than most women's clothing off the rack, and that was good because today she had to carry both her wallet and her phone in an interior pocket, and she carried her gun in a compression holster tank top. Like the tee she'd worn a couple of nights ago, the tank was designed to slim the line of a gun worn under clothing, and for work like this, Ellie appreciated it even more.

"Thank God," Khalil said when she found him backstage. "Can you hang out here for a couple of minutes? I'll be right back."

Pee break, Ellie guessed. "Sure. Anything in particular you need me to do?"

"Direct traffic as needed. Thanks." He darted away, and Ellie stood near the entrance off the stage, watching the controlled chaos that was a fashion show. Racks of clothing took up half the space, and nervous assistants flitted like birds through them, yelling at each other to hurry up and grab particular articles of clothing. Models discarded shoes and other outer layers then retreated behind several portable screens as they changed into yet another outfit. It was similar to a pit crew at a racing event.

"Ellie," came Tyler's voice over her headset. She clicked the switch on the cord to her headset.

"Go ahead."

"I'm at the main entrance and can't leave. Can you deliver something to Marya?"

"Is she in the audience still?"

"Yes."

Khalil reappeared, a look of utter relief on his face.

"On my way," she said to Tyler. "Gotta run," she said to Khalil.

"Thanks," he said just as someone raced up to him and demanded to know where the Evian was. Wow. Water meltdowns really were a thing at events like this.

"Marya needs something," Ellie said. "Can you handle this?"

He nodded, plastered on a big, fake smile, and pointed at the large portable drink cooler a few feet away that said "Evian" on the side. Ellie ducked out before she got pulled into something else and went quickly to the main entrance without cutting through the runway room. She found Tyler updating Liz and issuing instructions to others. When he saw her, he held up a finger to wait and she did. After a few seconds, he handed her a plain white envelope, unsealed.

"Get that to Marya now. Thanks."

Ellie took it and went backstage first, where she pulled the paper out and scanned it. Nothing that looked like gun specs or sales, so she slipped it back into the envelope and went to the runway room, where camera flashes were exploding like starlight. She worked her way around the perimeter until she was near the part of the stage where the models entered from the back. Marya was seated in the front, right next to the stage, about five seats in. Fortunately, there was room between these seats and the runway. Ellie waited for the cameras to stop, and at that point, all the models filed backstage. Ellie moved quickly to Marya's seat and leaned down to be heard.

"Delivery, Ms. Hampstead. From Tyler." She held the envelope out.

Marya looked up at her, gaze drilling into hers for a moment that heated Ellie's blood. Jesus, all Marya had to do was look at her and it caused all kinds of interesting sensations. Annoying, because there was nothing Ellie could do about it.

"Thank you." Marya took the envelope, and Ellie retreated before the next viewing started, but not before she realized that Lyev Koslov was seated in Marya's row, two people down.

Well, why not? Natalie was his cousin, after all. And he hung out with Marya sometimes. Though this was twice in a week after a few months of not spending time together. She took her phone out of her jacket and pretended to be checking messages on it. Instead, she filmed the audience near the stage before she went backstage in search of Natalie.

Christ, she'd been here since eight, and now it was almost three.

"Last showing," Khalil said when he saw her.

"Okay."

"Then there'll be some photo shoots, press, and some interviews. Tyler and the senior editorial staff handle that. Just be ready to be a gopher for whatever."

"Will do." Ellie checked the area backstage that Natalie Koslov had been using, and there she was, someone working on her hair while someone else dealt with her makeup. Her expression was placid, almost zen-like. The people stepped away, and she stood, already fully dressed in an outfit that looked sort of like a pink gunnysack with matching platform shoes. Nobody in their right mind would wear that anywhere outside this venue, but these models rocked every crazy thing they put on, in the exaggerated statements of the fashion world that trickled down in other shapes and forms to the masses.

Natalie straightened and walked toward the entrance to the stage. Khalil said that Natalie did "street" really well, which was a purposeful, focused walk that was supposed to evoke the streets of a big city. But on a runway, that kind of walk got little accents and personal touches added.

The music changed, and Natalie went onstage. An approving murmur rose from the crowd, along with a flood of camera flashes. Natalie was clearly one of the more popular models here.

A few minutes later, the show ended and backstage was flooded with models and assistants changing yet again to prepare for PR and interviews, if applicable. Within fifteen minutes, several long tables had been set up in the runway room and a few models were autographing photos, Natalie among them. Ellie stood just behind Natalie's table, prepared to give her water or another stack of photos or whatever her little model heart desired, but she also watched her sign, so she took her phone out and managed to film it.

With her marker, Natalie signed her stage name and then usually included a stylish little heart underneath it. Same thing, every time. Nothing there.

Damn.

Natalie finished at the table and got up to make room for someone else. Ellie kept her phone out and followed her as she worked her way through the crowd, smiling at various people. A well-dressed older man stopped and asked her a question. Natalie nodded and smiled, and he handed her a pen and a photo that looked like the ones she'd just been signing. This time, Natalie flipped the photo over and wrote something on the back. He smiled and handed her what looked like a business card. Ellie caught the entire exchange with her phone.

Holy shit. Was this how they did it? That fucking simple? Ellie watched as another well-dressed man approached and handed her yet another promo photo and a pen. She again wrote something on the back, smiled at him, and he exchanged the photo for a business card. She continued walking through the post-runway show crowd. Camera flashes exploded around her, and she posed for a moment before she handed something to Lyev that looked a lot like business cards. Ellie filed that away for future thought and decided to take her chances with the most recent autograph hound, so she followed him instead of Koslov.

First, these dudes had not been in line with everybody else to get signed photos. Second, they had brought their own photos for her to sign. And third, this one, at least, folded the photo and put it in his pocket and was now headed to the main entrance. Who did that? Folded an autographed photo?

Time for another Ellie O'Donnell special distraction. She followed him, grabbed a bottle of water off a nearby table, and unscrewed the top as she walked. She took her name tag off and slipped it into her inside jacket pocket.

"I don't care how you do it," she said loudly into her phone. "We don't have time for this." And...boom. She plowed right into Mr. Autograph, spilling a bit of water on the front of his suit. "Oh, shit," she said. "I'm so, so sorry. Let me get you a towel." She made a show of putting her phone back in her pocket before she screwed the top back on the bottle and set it on the floor as he brushed at the front of his suit.

He glared at her. "It'll dry," he said in an Eastern European accent. Ellie brushed at his suit, too, and held it open, pretending to inspect. "Seems it didn't soak through—better move this photo, though." She slid the photo of Natalie Koslov out of his inside jacket pocket, glad to see he'd folded it with the front side in, so she could get a quick look at the back.

He grabbed the photo out of her hand. "I'm fine," he said as he stalked out of the building. Ellie took her phone out and filmed him. And though he'd taken the photo away, she'd seen what Natalie had written, in easy-to-read block letters: *Love to H. Georgios in Red Hook, 26-9.*

She texted the info to Rick. "See image on vid. Sending in a bit." She then emailed the latest video she'd taken to him. So was the guy she'd bumped into H. Georgios? And what were the numbers? She picked up the bottle of water as her headset crackled.

"All hands on deck," Tyler said. "Meet me backstage for final PR help."

"Will do," she responded so he didn't have to contact her again. She went back into the fray, wondering who the hell H. Georgios was and what he had to do with arms deals. Maybe her idea had been a bust, and people just walked around with particular photos of models they wanted them to sign. But that didn't explain why he folded it. Creases ruined the photo. No, there was something about what Natalie had written that held meaning beyond a simple autograph. What that meaning was, however, eluded her, but she didn't have time to think about it once she got backstage.

CHAPTER 11

"Good job, today." Tyler smiled and handed Ellie a glass of champagne.

"Thanks." She took it and sipped.

"What did you think?"

"It's a lot more work than I thought. Kind of exciting. But also stressful."

He smiled and sipped his own champagne. "You're cool under pressure. Marya appreciates that."

"Good to know. I'll keep it up."

Somebody Ellie didn't know came up to Tyler and started talking to him. The distraction gave her a chance to look around at the people gathered for the reception, which was in a swanky private room above an equally swanky restaurant a few blocks from the event venue. The place was retro-aviation themed, with sleek steel accents on the walls that included strategically placed airplane propellers and tables and chairs that looked like they'd come out of first class in a 1960s airliner. So this was how the other half lived. Not bad. But not quite her thing, either.

Natalie and Lyev Koslov were on the other side of the room, chatting to each other and another group of beautiful people that included Marya. Ellie put her champagne glass on the tray of a passing server and went to the bar where she got a Coke. She'd never been a fan of champagne and besides, she wanted to stay focused. She went to the food table and loaded up on fruit and cheese. Rick would be proud of her. Well, maybe not for the cheese. She added a few vegetables and munched away, watching the crowd.

"Hi," Liz said.

"Hey. Tired?"

"Very. But it's always fun to meet some of the people who come to shows. And I took a bunch of photos. Ms. H liked a few of them," she said, a little awed.

"Congrats." Ellie felt her personal cell phone vibrate against her chest. "Maybe she'll use some of them in forthcoming issues."

"Oh, my God. That would be amazing."

Two guys Ellie recognized from Fashion Forward approached and started talking to Liz, which gave her time to set her plate down and check the text. Rick, wanting her to call him.

"Hi, honey," she said when he picked up. "How's your day been?"

"Never thought I'd hear that from you. Anyway, your photo guy is Czech, connected to arms dealing, too. And he appears to have a thing for fashion shows. He was at one in Paris and another in Milan, all within the past three months. And no, his name is not H. Georgios."

"Sounds good," she said. "Rain check on tonight. I'll catch up with you later. Bye." She hung up to the sound of him laughing. Her hunch had been right. So now they just needed to figure out who this Georgios dude was, where in Red Hook he happened to be, and how he figured in. All in all, a good day. She took her phone out and panned it around the room slowly then sent the video to Rick.

So far, she didn't see anybody she recognized beyond Koslov, Marya and staff, and a few of the models. No sign of Petrovs or Koslovs from the myriad mug shots she'd studied since this case started. There were family members on both sides who didn't have police records but might be involved in illegal activities. They just hadn't been caught yet.

Ellie finished off her plate of food. Knowing Marya and company, they'd probably go out to dinner and hold court there. She'd turn surveillance back over to the team once that happened, and then she'd go home and get caught up on some sleep—

Hello. Things might have just gotten interesting. Lyev and Natalie Koslov peeled off from the crowd and were on their way toward the restaurant downstairs. Ellie followed, pretending to talk on her phone.

Lyev and Natalie went down the tight metal spiral staircase to the restaurant and walked to a table in the corner near the main entrance, where somebody else sat, partially obscured.

Think fast. Ah. She grabbed a couple of menus off a nearby server station and walked toward the table, trying to look all hostess-like, even stopping to inquire about people's meals at a couple of other tables. Too bad this wasn't on film. Oscar-worthy, no doubt. She was finally close enough to see the other person at the table.

Jonathan Hampstead.

Ellie diverted to another table to inquire about the meal before he saw her. Probably not a good idea to go take their orders. She went back to the server station, took a photo of the table in the back corner, and texted it to Rick, with the names of the occupants since the photo probably sucked. That was one thing she really wasn't that good at. She left the menus and went back up the stairs. Did Marya know her dad was here? What the hell with her dad, talking to Natalie Koslov, who was probably involved in gun-running? This shit kept getting weirder. As she went back up the stairs, she almost ran into Tyler, who was on his way down.

"There you are," he said. "You've been invited to an after party in upper Manhattan."

She stared up at him, since he was higher up on the stairs.

"It's at a private residence, but lots of fashionistas, as they say, will be there."

"Is that okay with Marya—Ms. H?" Oops. She'd referred to the Empress by her first name.

Tyler smiled. "She invited you."

Well. That settled that. "Sounds great. Just tell me where to go."

"Not to worry. You'll be in our car. We're leaving in about fifteen." He spun and went back up the stairs and Ellie followed. At the top, she texted Rick with the new info. And then she thought about the fact that Marya had invited her to this party. So she was now in the ice queen's good graces? It felt like it after the pub. But maybe Marya was capricious. And maybe Ellie didn't care, because this was about the case.

Right?

The case, dammit. Think about the case. She put her phone back into her jacket pocket and went into the reception room.

Ellie stared out the windows of this apartment, which took up an entire floor of a high rise. This is what the other half paid for, incredible views like this. And gajillion-dollar apartments in upper Manhattan that looked like they should be featured in *Architectural Digest*. Hell, for all she knew, this one was. The guy who owned it worked in investments. He also happened to own a couple of modeling agencies and was some muckety-muck with Gloria Vanderbilt.

She sipped her drink—special dispensation from Rick again to blend in. This was another reason she was going to be sad when this assignment was over, because she would not be invited to venues like this. She turned and looked at the knots of people standing around and chatting. Lyev and Natalie had arrived later than she had, and there was no sign of Jonathan Hampstead. She'd done rounds twice already and listened to their conversations for a while, but it was all fashion and celebrity shop talk and nothing that sounded even remotely like they were about to run guns out of Russia into global hot spots.

Marya had spent the entire ride to the party talking on the phone, but she was polite about it, and Ellie, who sat across from her in the limo, pretended to care about what Liz was saying about her photos when what she was really doing was admiring the view of cleavage she got when Marya moved a certain way. Her hair was up today, and she wore a black pants suit with a pale yellow blouse that Ellie was dying to take off her. There was nothing on this earth that wouldn't look good on Marya Hampstead. Probably nothing on this earth that wouldn't look good off her, either.

Thinking about that caused aches in parts of Ellie's anatomy that tried to override her rationality. Work the case, she reminded herself. So she engaged with some of Marya's staff she hadn't really talked to and worked her way around the room. One thing she'd learned from Gwen was how to do this convincingly, though Rick had told her that she was a natural social butterfly. Gwen had just brought it out.

A few people had retreated to a balcony to smoke and admire the view, and Ellie joined them since she'd probably never get a chance to hang out at a place like this again. The breeze blew the cigarette smoke away, and low murmurs of people chatting actually proved relaxing after today. Jesus, she was tired. Fashion was hard. Fashion combined with arms deals was even harder. And all of that combined with a woman as intriguing as Marya Hampstead—shit, she needed at least a month to recover.

The night added a chill to the air, and Ellie was glad she had worn a jacket today, even though she'd practically melted at the fashion show. She leaned on the railing, enjoying the view even more.

"So how did your first event go?" Marya's voice right next to Ellie sent sparks of pleasure down her legs.

"I think pretty well," she said, glad she sounded smooth. She turned her head to look at Marya. "Though it did get a little insane at times."

"Tyler said you have a knack for calming things down." Marya gazed out over the Hudson, and took a sip from her glass.

"That's nice of him." She wasn't sure why he'd say that. She hadn't done anything out of the ordinary.

"Refreshing, in this line of work." Marya leaned on the railing.

"You're saying that people tend to be high-strung in this industry?"

"Not in so many words." There was a smile in her tone as she caught Ellie's gaze in the light that spilled through the balcony doors. A strand of hair blew into Marya's face. She moved it with a graceful gesture, and that made Ellie burn like a woman left in a desert's blazing sun.

"It's been refreshing having you around," Marya said.

She forgot to breathe. Instead, she took another drink. When in doubt, drink from the glass you're holding.

"What are your plans after your time with us ends?"

She sipped again before answering, as if thinking about it. "Hopefully a job in the industry. But if not, there's always ad copy. I'll figure something out." Oh, another Oscar in her future, for this performance, for sure.

"And how has your experience with us been so far?"

"Honestly, it's been a lot more fun than I thought it would be."

Marya smiled, and it only added to the slow burn between her thighs and all up and down her spine. "Why is that?" she asked.

"I've met some interesting people and done some interesting things. Plus, you liked my Agent Carter idea."

At that, Marya chuckled. Oh, God. Ellie checked her glass. She still had whiskey left. Thankfully.

"There are lots of rumors about me," she said, staring out over the Hudson again. "And you no doubt have heard them. Yet you applied for the internship anyway."

"I have thick skin." The whiskey was warm on her tongue and tangy. And it didn't help at all, because all she was thinking about right now was how Marya's tongue would taste and feel in her mouth.

"So I've noticed." Marya pushed off the railing. "I particularly like how you interact with me."

She gave Marya her full attention.

"You're definitely not the starstruck type, and you have no idea how nice I find that."

"Glad to hear it."

"And I could make a position for you. Now, if you'd like." She paused.

Ellie waited for her to continue.

"But I find I'm reluctant to offer one."

She stared at her, not sure where this was going. So Marya would hire her, but not? She was suddenly aware that it was only the two of them out here, on this balcony in the September night.

And then Marya stepped closer, until there was barely a foot between them. "I have a policy, Ms. Daniels."

"Ellie," she said automatically, her heart pounding. "A policy about what?"

"If I hire you, then I can't act on this interesting attraction I have for you."

Wait. What? Somebody needed to do a rewind, because she was almost sure that Marya Hampstead just said she was attracted to her. But shit like that didn't happen in the real world. Except that Marya was toying with her tie, and she was standing so close she could feel her body heat.

"And I'd like to act on it, eventually." Marya stared into her eyes, and Ellie wondered, if she got a running start, whether she could jump far enough out to actually hit the Hudson, because she definitely needed a cooling down. How did Marya not see the flames shooting out of the top of her head?

"I'm glad you told me about this policy," Ellie said, fighting the urge to pull her into a kiss to end all kisses, and she sounded like her regular self, thank God.

"Oh? Why?"

"Because I would be so fired right now for my actions if I didn't know about it."

She smiled again. "Then we understand each other."

"I'd say so."

"Good. We can revisit later." She let go of Ellie's tie and stepped away. "Have a good evening, Ellie. See you Monday."

"You, too."

Marya turned and headed back inside, but she stopped at the threshold and looked at her again. "Call me Marya." And then she stepped inside and was gone.

Ellie was pretty sure her jaw had bounced off her face and fallen right off the balcony. Except she checked, and no, it was still attached to her face. How was this even happening?

And hello, but she had a case to break.

And it might involve busting *the* Marya Hampstead. Who, as it turned out, had a thing for the ladies. Not just any lady. Her. Ellie, who was working for her under false pretenses.

She groaned softly and finished her whiskey.

CHAPTER 12

This was probably her twentieth piece of cinnamon candy. Rick might be right, that they were going to kill her, because her teeth kind of hurt. Could teeth hurt? Maybe they hurt because she'd been clenching them together since last night, thinking about what Marya had said to her.

This had to be a dream. Totally. Marya Hampstead hated everybody.

Didn't she?

It sure didn't feel like it last night.

Fuck. She got up to get another cup of coffee. She was at her desk on a Sunday, trying to figure out who H. Georgios was. So far, nothing. Not a damn thing.

Rick looked up from his own desk when she walked past. "You hungry?"

"Damn right."

"I'll buy you lunch, since you've spent so much time with the ice queen."

If he only knew. "I'll totally let you."

"Greek okay?'

"I love you."

He laughed. "Save it for Ms. Right."

"How about Ms. Right Now?"

"That'll do. I'm ordering now. Your usual?"

She laughed. "Yes. And clearly, we spend far too much time together if you know what that is."

"Hey, I pay attention."

"Honey, I didn't know you cared." She made fake kissy noises at him.

"Stow it. You've done some great work. Nobody figured it was models until you took the assignment." He started to order online. "Should I get a couple of Cokes for you?"

"I'm serious, dude. We should probably just get married and call it done."

"Don't tempt me. Cokes it is."

"What? I'm kind of cute. You'd have a cute wife for work functions." She batted her eyelashes at him.

"Save it, O'Donnell. You're smokin' hot, even without all the fashion overhauls."

"Aw. You noticed." She unwrapped another candy and put it in her mouth. "I could deal with you. You're clean, for a dude. You take care of yourself. And you dress nice. I like the mix of natural fabrics. Plus, you smell good."

He looked at her with his "wtf" expression. "Seriously?"

"We're a good match. And your mom likes me."

He laughed again. "And she knows you're not straight. Plus, she keeps hoping I'll find somebody like Beyoncé, in terms of looks and business smarts."

"Fine. I'll settle for having you as a work husband. Take that, Queen Bey."

"You're too much." He looked back at his monitor, and she stared at her laptop, at the hundredth search she'd done on H. Georgios, in a dozen different databases and across myriad search engines and tools. What the hell was she missing?

"Fuck," she muttered. "Who is this guy?"

"Food should be here in twenty," Rick said. "Let's talk about Natalie."

"Cool. What've you got?" She pushed back from her desk, holding her coffee in one hand.

"So, at her last show in Moscow, she was approached by a gentleman who has ties to arms dealings in Turkey."

"Who?"

"Another businessman who passed her a photo to sign."

"Do we know what it said on the back?"

"Kind of. The informant didn't get the look that you did, but he remembers another name. Dimitriov."

"Did the guy pass her a business card?"

"The informant didn't say. We ran the name he provided against the Koslovs and the Petrovs and got nothing that has anything to do with what we're looking for."

"Did the informant notice any numbers on it?"

"Something like fifteen-eight."

"What about a place?"

"Didn't see."

Ellie stared at the ceiling. "They have to be dates. Maybe times. But for what? And where else has Natalie been that she was approached by others?"

"Checking. It was random, this tip from Moscow. The tipster thought it was weird that somebody would approach her with his own publicity shot for signing."

"Yeah, same here. Did he follow the businessman?"

Rick made a disgusted noise in the back of his throat.

"I'm guessing that's a no," Ellie said as she rolled her chair back to her desk. "Okay, then." She checked her desk drawer. She was definitely going to need more candy. So how about just doing some searches in Red Hook? Russians and Greeks, since the name she'd seen on the back of the photo was Greek. Besides, it kept her focused on the case and not thinking about what Marya had said to her the night before. Until right now. Dammit. Focus.

Twenty minutes later she stopped. Another big, fat nothing. Rick got up and left. Even on a Sunday, he wore a nice shirt and trousers. Some straight woman would be only too glad to get a hold of that. He returned a few minutes later with a bag of food. Ellie could smell it before she could see him and realized she was hungrier than she thought.

"All right. Souvlaki for our resident fashion queen." He took a styrofoam container out and placed it on her desk. "Two Cokes. Extra pita."

"I meant what I said, bro. I love you." She dug in before he even sat down at his own desk. While she ate, she kept trying different combinations of searches in different database. "This is so good. Thanks," she said a few minutes later. "And it always tastes fresh, like they shipped it in this morning—" she stopped, several things clicking into place in her brain.

He looked over at her. "You okay?"

"Shipped," she said.

He gave her another of his "wtf" looks.

"Right there. The whole time. Shipping. They're the names of *ships*. What the hell else would illegal arms come in on?"

He stared at her. "Fuck." And then he was typing things on his keyboard. "Holy Mary, Joseph, and Jesus," he said after a few seconds.

"That's mighty Catholic of you."

"I'll be Catholic if it solves this case. And look. *H. Georgios*," he said. "The *Hellas Georgios*, scheduled to arrive at the Red Hook Container Terminal Tuesday night at ten-thirty."

"Holy shit. Twenty-six-nine. That's how people who aren't American write dates. The day first, then the month." Ellie took a swig of soda.

"That's got to be it. I'm guessing the guy at the event yesterday put in an order with Koslov and his dude on the other end wires the money to a European account."

"So is the ship bringing arms in or taking them out?" Ellie took another bite. In spite of all the excitement, she was still hungry.

"Not sure. If they're bringing them in, then maybe the buyers move them to other ships and send them along. Maybe the containers just sit there on the pier for a while until the Koslovs round up buyers."

"Which means there're people on the piers that are involved."

He nodded. "Speaking of, we've had a tail on Jonathan Hampstead since last night."

"Oh? What's he up to?"

"Meetings at banks. Seems legit."

She snorted. "Please. He's probably in Red Hook right now killing the fuck out of people on the pier where the *Georgios* is scheduled to dock."

He laughed so hard that, once he was done, he had to take a drink of water. "We already checked," he managed. "He is, in fact, in banking meetings. But I do appreciate the image."

She finished one of the pitas that had come with her meal. "I want in on this."

He swiveled in his chair to look at her. "Surveillance op. If we can get evidence on film of arms dealing, then we can follow it and see how deep this shit goes. And yes, you're going because if anybody shows up from Fashion Forward, you can ID them. But you're going to stay with the team."

"I want to be on the docks."

"We'll see."

"When will this happen?"

"We'll scope it out today and tomorrow, and if it's a go, we'll start setting up Tuesday morning. As for you, go to Fashion Forward like usual. Leave around lunch on Tuesday and go to the apartment and we'll get you wired up and ready."

She nodded and took a bite of the other pita.

"And check this out. The *Dimitriov* is another cargo vessel. It docked in Red Hook August fifteenth," he said. "Fifteen-eight, European date style."

"So Natalie gets the ships and dock dates of the arms and passes them to buyers at fashion shows. And they hand her a card with whatever info for her records and Lyev's. That's slick."

"Where there's smoke, there's fire. There have to be other models involved."

And probably fashion moguls, Ellie thought, dread filling her gut like bad Chinese food. She needed to get over this. Whatever she felt for Marya Hampstead, it was just an attraction. Tons of people were attracted to Marya, after all. She cultivated that. But she'd also admitted an attraction for Ellie, and nobody in the world had yet figured out that Marya had a thing for women, too, so that was something, that Marya had trusted her with it.

Did that mean anything? Or did she know that because Ellie was basically a nobody on the fashion circuit that nobody would believe her for a minute if Marya took her to bed?

Oh, God. *There* was an image that made her almost pass out. But seriously, maybe she took women to bed all the time. Maybe she picked women who were nobodies on the circuit so she could get away with it. And sitting here, thinking about her, Ellie would totally let her do it. She opened the other Coke and took a long drink. Focus. They were so close to maybe breaking parts of this case.

So how come she was dreading it?

It didn't matter. This was her job. Nothing personal. She finished her food in silence while Rick called the rest of the team and doled out instructions. They'd only just clued in to what was going on, and they'd want to figure out as much as they could about who was involved, where the arms went, and they'd alert officials overseas, and it would go on for a while. All of that ran through Ellie's head. As did the fact that Marya didn't want to hire her on, which would put a crimp in the operation. And Ellie would have to tell Rick that she'd gotten closer to Marya than she should have, and that was a problem.

Of course, Rick might think it was great, and he might encourage her to hook up with Marya to get even closer, and get even more information.

And that made her feel even worse, because she was genuinely attracted to her, and she hated the thought of passing information along in a situation like that. Even if Marya herself had popped those Petrovs, Ellie was having a hard time seeing past the ice queen's not-so-icy eyes and her teasing little smiles.

This was so fucked up.

She finished her food and decided to wait until after the *Georgios* docked. At that point, she'd re-assess where things were with the investigation and see what role she should play. She was not looking forward to it.

CHAPTER 13

Ellie finished making another cup of coffee and was on the way back to her office when Tyler intercepted her.

"We've got some mock-ups on the proofs that we're looking over. Are you interested?"

"Sure." She followed him, and instead of the conference room where she'd had her first meeting, they went to Marya's office. The door was open, and Tyler walked right in. She brushed at her blouse, as if there might be some kind of lint ball clinging to the fabric, and went in. She wore trousers today again because the bruise on her shin was the size of a softball, but she had opted for heels.

"Have a seat," Tyler said, pointing at Marya's table. Khalil was there, but no sign of Marya.

"Hi," he said.

She nodded a greeting and sat down across from him.

"So..." Tyler spread the mock-ups out over the table, "here we go. They need some tweaking, but this is basically where we're going."

"The font needs a little work here and here." Khalil pointed. "But I like the placement of the images. It's kind of retro, but not."

She looked them over. It was cool, to see an idea she'd thrown out transformed into something like this.

"There is still work to be done," Marya said as she entered, and a little jolt of pleasure went up Ellie's spine.

"Having said that, I admit that I'm pleased with this first run." She took the seat directly to Ellie's right, at the head of the table. "What do you think, Ellie?" she asked.

Ellie looked at her, surprised that she'd referred to her by her first name.

"I like that it has a Forties movie-poster feel, but with an upgrade. Kind of a merging of retro and modern, like Khalil just said. And the colors—I like how you notice them, but they're not overwhelming." She had this lingo down.

"I haven't seen anything quite like this elsewhere," Tyler said. "So it will be noticed."

"Good." Marya sat back, and Ellie wrenched her gaze to the layouts. Marya looked far too hot in that deep red blouse. "Let's pay attention to what the competition is doing over the next few issues. Whatever it is, we will do it better." She stood. "Thank you. And now, I have a lunch date. Tyler, I want to meet with you and design at two. These—" she motioned at the layouts—"need to be done today."

He nodded and gathered them up, and Ellie stood and followed the guys out, overheated even from this brief encounter with Marya. But she had a damn job to do, so she checked the time on her phone. Almost twelve. She went back to the coffee room and pretended to be waiting in line while she watched the corridor that led to Marya's office.

A few moments later, Marya strode across the lobby alone, and people murmured greetings to her as she passed, walking like an empress on her way to a state function. She exited through the glass doors to the outer lobby area where the elevators were, and at that point, one of her security guards got up from a bench and tapped the down button for her. They both entered when it arrived.

Ellie went back to her office and shut the door. She called Rick.

"Yeah."

"She's got a lunch date. On the way down with one security guard."

"On it. Out." He hung up, and she waited fifteen minutes before she picked up a few papers from her desk along with her phone and returned to Marya's office. The door was closed. She tried the handle. It was unlocked. After a quick glance to make sure nobody was around, she slipped in and shut it behind her.

She set the papers on the table and moved to Marya's desk, which was one of those Swedish design things, all metal and glass, but there were a few drawers. Ellie tried them all and they were all unlocked. She glanced through. Marya kept organized but mostly empty desk drawers. A few pens, a couple of blank scratch pads, and a stash of British tea bags. She smiled at that. It gave Marya another humanizing touch. She picked up the scratch pads and examined them for impressions. It didn't look as if they'd been used.

Was everything Marya did online? No files? No instructions for meeting the international arms dealers? No gun inventory? Why couldn't potential criminals make this shit easy?

Her desk was an expanse of organization. A plain metal penholder that also held scissors. There was also a lamp that matched the desk, and Marya's laptop. She checked the recycling and trash containers, as well. Then she tapped the space key on Marya's laptop and the password screen came up. Dammit. No international gun inventory right there on her desktop to see. Ellie checked the time on her phone. She'd been in here for about ten minutes. She got up and put the chair back the way she'd found it and went to the closet, which was also unlocked.

Not much in here beyond an umbrella and two long overcoats. One looked like a winter coat. Ellie checked the pockets on both and came up with a couple of cough drops and a pack of Kleenex. Kind of cute, that a fashion empress would carry stuff like that in her coat.

Somebody knocked at the door, and she ducked into the closet, which was barely big enough for her. She pulled the door almost closed, keeping it cracked so she could watch the main door.

Tyler entered, with what looked like layout sheets. He set them on the table then turned to go but stopped and looked at something else on the table. Ellie opened the door a tiny bit wider. Shit. The papers she'd brought from her office. What was on them? Anything identifying?

He moved a couple of them, as if trying to figure out whose they were, then left, shutting the door behind him. She exhaled in relief but stayed put for a couple of minutes, just in case, and leaned back against Marya's coats. She thought she could still smell a bit of her cologne on them. Wishful thinking, probably. This boundary between stalker and investigator was woefully permeable, especially with this damn attraction thing.

She stepped back into the main office, closet jokes running through her head, and gathered the papers she'd brought in before she cracked the door to the corridor. A few people walked past, talking, and she waited a couple of seconds before she stepped out of Marya's office and closed the door just as someone rounded the corner from the lobby. Ellie knocked on the door and made a show of listening.

"I think she went to lunch," the woman said who approached her.

"Oh. I didn't realize. Thanks." She moved away from the door with a smile. Her phone buzzed with a text. Rick, wanting her to call him ASAP. She decided she should grab lunch, too, so she dropped her papers off at her office and went down to the main lobby and then outside to call.

"Hey," she said when he picked up.

"Marya's having lunch with Daddy."

"Where?"

"Uptown. There was a car waiting for her when she came downstairs."

Of course there was. She leaned against the building. "Does it look legit? Like, you know, meeting in a public place and just hanging out?"

"Or are they plotting world domination and random murders, you mean?"

"Yeah. I guess. What does that look like, when you're doing that?"

"Probably like you're not doing it. So that might be exactly what they're up to."

"Or they're just having lunch," Ellie said, though she didn't believe it. "Any sign of Laskin, by the way?"

"Nope."

"Do me a favor. Run him and whatever aliases we have on him against fashion shows. See if anything comes up."

"See? I knew you'd be perfect for this assignment. Out."

She hung up. Nothing in Marya's office. Maybe she kept stuff at home. But that was a whole other issue, searching that. Or maybe, if she was an arms dealer, she was just freaking careful about everything, and left nothing to chance. Maybe she had hidden hard drives all over the world that only she could access. And maybe Ellie should just go to lunch right now, because she was starting to sound like a *Bourne* movie again. Maybe Chinese today.

The dark, hulking shape of the *Hellas Georgios* moved slowly toward the pier, its deck stacked three to five levels high with different colored containers the size of boxcars. Lights blazed as a crane slowly swung into position, getting ready for the unloading. Even at night, this place was like a beehive. Ellie sniffed, catching the odors of river muck and diesel fuel in the breeze.

She stood watching as the ship prepared to dock, port side to the pier, which in itself was a hell of a feat. The thrum of its engines drowned out a lot of sound this close to the pier, and she adjusted her hard hat so she could pull the knit cap down over her ears and earpiece, as if that would help. One of the team members stood nearby, talking to the Port Authority guy working with them. He had gotten them in here for the night shift.

Rick hadn't been thrilled with her request to get this close to the action, but he'd relented when she dressed up in her longshore outfit—black cargo pants, beat-up work boots, and dark tee and flannel shirt. A dark work jacket and knit cap completed her ensemble, along with a hard hat, and he agreed that she looked more like a young guy than a woman in this outfit. Besides, she could identify people from Marya's inner circle at Fashion Forward if they ended up here.

Somehow, she doubted they would. And she really, really hoped that Marya wasn't here. Nobody actually knew where she was. She hadn't come in to work, and Rick had called the main number to see if he could find out when she'd be in next. He'd talked to Tyler, who said that Marya was on a business trip to Boston, back on Friday. Ellie wondered if that was true, or if it's just what Marya wanted Tyler to believe.

The Port Authority guy started to move closer to the ship, still talking to the team member. Ellie tagged along, looking like the new guy Mr. Port Authority had said she was. This close, the ship was massive, like a horizontal skyscraper or some gigantic lumbering water beast, as it finally was close enough to anchor and get tied down. Docking ships like this in confined waters like Red Hook was a feat, and it had been almost an hour since the ship had arrived. A pilot tug aided the procedure. It had pulled close and disgorged a second pilot, who climbed up a ladder to the deck. This procedure was difficult enough that there needed to be a pilot aiding the captain.

She checked her watch. Almost midnight, and so far, no sign of anybody she recognized. This was probably going to be a bust and they'd be no closer to figuring out what the hell was going on.

And she still had to figure out how to navigate the waters around Marya.

"Els," came Rick's voice through her earpiece. "We've got another tugboat on the starboard side."

"Copy that," she said softly. She dropped back and moved farther away from the ship, trying to get a better angle. Yes, there was indeed another tugboat in the water that had pulled up near the pilot tug. "Looks like a pilot boat," she said. And then she just made out what looked like two dark shapes that left the boat and climbed up the same ladder the pilot had a half-hour ago. "Movement. One, possibly two more boarding the ship."

The *Georgios* was finally being tethered, and the gangplank lowered, so Ellie went toward that. She glanced around for her team members, but didn't see them in the knots of people preparing to unload. She moved closer to the ship, checking the crowd, and caught sight of a familiar face, but not one she expected.

"Yuri Laskin is here," she said.

"Are you sure?" Rick asked through her earpiece.

"I blendered the dude's knee. Of course I'm sure. And I'm ten feet away." She moved a little closer. Definitely Laskin.

The ship's crew and dock workers secured the gangplank—which was more a portable staircase along the ship's side—and Laskin walked toward it. She followed him, keeping a safe distance between them.

"Laskin is boarding," she said as he started up the steps. "I'm going in."

"Wait," came Rick's voice. "O'Donnell—"

"Give me ten minutes to find out who he's meeting."

"Let me get backup into position—"

"No time. He's almost to the deck. Going to observe." She was at the foot of the gangplank. No time like the present, so she ascended, hoping she looked like she fit in. She made it to the deck without anyone commenting, either from below or above, so she continued to act like she belonged, and strode purposefully away from the stairs and moved quickly into the maze of stacked containers, which weren't as much of a labyrinth as she thought.

They had been loaded with narrow passages between the rows, but if someone was claustrophobic, this was definitely not a place to be. With lights ablaze on the ship and the dock, though, it wasn't as creepy or claustrophobic as it might have been. She moved between two high rows of containers toward the starboard side, playing a hunch that Laskin was headed toward the people who had come aboard after the pilot did.

She had to be close to the starboard side by now. Somebody was talking up ahead, and she moved forward slowly, trying to listen. From the cadence of the voices, it was an intense—angry?—conversation. She heard a thump and a grunt and then the clang of metal on metal. She drew her own pistol and peered carefully out from between the containers. Two guys were beating the hell out of each other a dozen feet away.

One of the guys hauled the other up and slammed him against a container. The guy who got slammed was big, and he punched the other guy and said something that sounded a lot like Russian. Ellie stayed put, and then the smaller guy body-slammed the bigger guy, and the latter stumbled backward and landed face-up so close to Ellie that she could have touched him. Even in the dim light, Ellie recognized Lyev Koslov.

The other guy hurled himself on top of Koslov. Something glinted in his hand. A knife. He shifted and...Laskin. Shit just went completely sideways, and she acted on instinct. She tossed her hard hat off to keep it from obstructing her vision and stepped out from between the containers.

"Freeze," she said in a hard, clear tone as she leveled her gun at Laskin's temple.

He stopped, surprised. Koslov did, too, from his position on the deck, and all three of them seemed to be holding a collective breath when a voice Ellie knew only too well sounded behind her.

"Hands up," Marya said.

Her heart sank into her knees. Hell.

"Please," Marya added.

She almost laughed out loud at that. So polite, the British. "Well," she said as she put her hands up. "*This* is awkward." She relaxed her fingers so Marya could take her gun.

"But you do have good taste in weapons," Marya said. And then she added something in Russian—Jesus, she spoke Russian, too?—and Laskin got off Koslov and dropped the knife. He put his hands up. Koslov then got up and picked up Laskin's knife.

"I see we've had a change in plans," said someone else and Ellie recognized Jonathan Hampstead's voice. She turned her head. Both Marya and Jonathan were dressed in dark clothing and Marya looked like a natural, holding both guns.

"Slightly. Turn this way, please," she said to Ellie.

She did, hoping that Rick could hear what was happening.

"Thank you," Jonathan said as he zip cuffed her wrists. After that, he removed Ellie's earpiece and stomped it on the deck. Then he checked all her pockets and pulled out her work cell and stomped that on the deck, too. Three rhythmic times, as if that was a magic stomping number for phones. He picked up the wreckage of the earpiece and the phone and put them in his jacket pocket.

Shit was not only sideways, it was completely blown out of the water.

Jonathan zip cuffed Laskin, too. Marya said something else to Koslov and gestured at the starboard side of the ship. Ellie recognized his response as an affirmative.

Jonathan stepped back a few paces with Marya, and they exchanged a hurried conversation. When it was over, he addressed Ellie.

"Now we're going to go down a ladder. I'll be right beneath you. If you try anything, or shout, I'll have you know it's hard to swim in cuffs, especially after you fall a few dozen meters into cold water. Is that clear?"

"Crystal," she said, and she glanced at Marya, who was studying her, sizing her up.

"Excellent. I'll go first." To Marya, he said, "Take care of this." And he switched one of her guns with a pistol and silencer. That couldn't be good. She didn't have time to ponder who was going to get the business end of that because Jonathan pushed her along the ship's walkway a couple dozen feet and stopped. Marya was right behind her, Ellie knew. And she had two guns, one with a silencer. Oh, shit. Would she use it on her?

If that was the case, why not just shoot her on the deck? She relaxed a little. They wouldn't have wasted time cuffing her and having her leave the ship if that was the deal.

She waited for Jonathan to swing himself onto the ladder that she knew would take them down to the second tugboat below.

Marya's hand was on Ellie's shoulder, and she pushed her gently toward the ladder. Ellie managed to get herself onto it, but this was not going to be easy, going down a ladder with her wrists like this. Slowly, she started down, Jonathan's hand at the small of her back. Marya watched them for a few seconds, her gaze locked onto Ellie's, and then she moved away from the ladder. It was just Ellie and Daddy Hampstead on a ladder at least fifty feet above the water.

Should she just go for it? Try to swim with zip cuffs? She'd been able to make it almost a quarter-mile once like that, but she hadn't been wearing this much clothing. That should be a new requirement for training, she thought. Being able to swim with zip cuffs while dressed as a longshoreman.

She lowered herself another couple of rungs, knowing that she could probably kick Jonathan right in the face and make him take a dip. But then what? Then she'd be stuck on this ladder, and Marya would shoot her or knock her into the water, too. At least she would be polite about it. "*Pardon me, Ellie. I must shoot you now. Cheers.*"

After what seemed like at least another hour but was probably only about ten minutes, Jonathan stopped. Ellie's shoulders ached from the slow, awkward way she'd had to descend.

"Well done," he said. "I'm going to pull you onto another boat. Please do not resist. Remember, the water is cold."

She let him help her onto the deck of a tugboat and at that point, he pulled out a roll of masking tape.

"Seriously?" she said.

"Yes." And he taped her mouth and led her below deck to a small room where he removed her zip cuffs but applied another set, this time with her arms behind her back. He also had her sit on the floor so he could zip cuff her ankles, then he turned off the light and shut the door behind him, its click loud and ominous in the dark.

Shit. She lay still for a few moments, remembering the layout of the room before Jonathan turned the lights out. There were two typical narrow crew bunks bolted into the back wall. There was a porthole opposite her and once her eyes adjusted, she could see part of the Manhattan skyline. A very narrow, constricted part, but at least it helped her to orient herself.

She hadn't seen anything else in here, but if she had to, she could probably work her way onto the bottom bunk and get a little more comfortable. She groaned behind the tape.

Rick was going to be so pissed at her.

CHAPTER 14

Within about ten minutes, the tug's engines started. It was hard for Ellie to tell if they were actually moving, but she got the sense they were. She glanced at the porthole. The view was slightly different. They were definitely moving. The engine's vibrations came up through the floor as the boat picked up speed.

She adjusted her position, still seated against the wall, and debated if she should try to somehow work her hands to her front so she could get the tape off her mouth. She'd done it once before, but it had taken her a while, and it hadn't been a pleasant experience. Well, why not? Might as well. She moved again to get into a better position but someone opened the door and turned on the light. She squinted in the sudden change. Marya kneeled in front of her, dressed in black BDUs, boots, and sweater. Oh, hell. Did she have the pistol with the silencer?

"Don't move," she said, and her fingers brushed Ellie's cheeks. "I'm taking the tape off."

Marya wouldn't do that if she was going to pop her. Ellie braced for the sting of the tape, but it was minimal. Thank God Jonathan used masking instead of duct tape. Marya tossed it onto the floor and pulled a folding knife out of her pocket. The blade clicked as she flicked it open. She cut the zip cuffs on Ellie's ankles, and Ellie moved so she could reach her wrists. She sighed with relief when the pressure of the cuffs released, and she rubbed her wrists but stayed seated, not sure what Marya would do next.

"Sorry about that." Marya handed her a bottle of water. She was still on one knee.

Ellie drank. "Thanks," she said, opting to use British-like manners. Perhaps that would ensure the dragon lady wouldn't stab her to death. Or shoot her. She screwed the top back on the bottle.

"Listen carefully," Marya said in a low voice. She was still on one knee in front of her. "I'm with a non-US agency. This is an op. We've been working for months on breaking an arms smuggling ring."

Ellie stared at her. She might have been less shocked had Marya actually turned into a dragon lady.

"I'm guessing that's probably what you're trying to do, but though we're on your side, we have to keep up appearances or everybody's cover is blown to hell."

She kept her mouth shut. An op? Who the hell was Marya Hampstead?

The noise from the boat's engines decreased. They were slowing down. Marya checked her watch.

"Give us fifteen minutes before you contact your team, and stay hidden. We're going to say you escaped."

Ellie nodded, wondering how Marya had figured out she even had a team. It hadn't even been thirty minutes since the *Georgios*. She started to get up, but her legs were numb. Marya helped her, and her hands were warm. Ellie let go of her fingers once she was standing because even in this completely bizarre situation, she liked how it felt to hold Marya's hands.

"Take a sick day tomorrow from Fashion Forward," Marya said, "since you're not going to get much sleep tonight. I'm ostensibly in Boston the rest of this week."

The engines stopped. Ellie rubbed her wrists again. "And tell my team what, exactly?"

"Don't worry. We'll brief them in a bit. We just can't do it now." She checked her watch again. "I have to go." She pulled Ellie's gun out of her waistband and handed it to her, butt-first. Hardly the actions of an international arms dealer with a cop in captivity. Unless she was pulling off the best double-cross ever. If so, Ellie would totally give up her pretend Oscar because Marya's performance had hers beat by a mile.

"You sure know how to show a girl a good time," she said wryly as she took the gun and checked the safety before she holstered it.

Marya smiled. "So do you." And then she leaned in and, holy Christ, pressed her lips against Ellie's, warm and soft, but fleeting. She was gone before Ellie could say anything else. Instead, she stood in the center of the tiny room, her mouth tingling, and stared at the door Marya had shut behind her. She snapped back to reality and checked her watch and waited. From above, she heard the slap of something on the water, and then another engine, this one an outboard. Marya and friends must have abandoned the boat with a raft. The engine noise faded into the distance.

She continued to wait, thoughts roiling. Jonathan had cuffed Laskin on the *Georgios*, which meant Koslov was in with Marya. Or did it? Hell, they'd cuffed her, though from what Marya had said, it was for appearances. Was cuffing Laskin for that, too? And who did Jonathan want Marya to take care of with the pistol and silencer? Her money was on Laskin. Or was he the guy who was key to this whole operation, and Jonathan cuffed him because finally, they'd caught him?

This was like a house of mirrors, and she still wasn't sure if Marya was legit or pulling a fast one. A fashion mogul who was also—what? CIA? Interpol? MI6? Alternatively, she was a total con artist. Ellie's gut said that wasn't the case, and she decided to go with that and take Marya at her word.

And lips.

Jesus, her lips.

She checked her watch and went upstairs to the bridge. There, she radioed Port Authority and settled in for another wait. And probably an ass-chewing from Rick. She sighed.

>|——•—••+•••—••+•••—•+•••—•|<

"What the fuck, O'Donnell?"

She stared at a spot on the wall. Rick never used her last name with that tone unless he was pissed or upset. Or both. This sounded like both.

"This whole fucking op may have just been blown from here to fucking hell. I told you to wait." He glared at her, hands on his hips. "And I don't fucking know if I can keep your ass out of the fire."

Shit. Suspension, probably. Write-up. She kept her mouth shut, knowing that her usual snark was not the way to play this.

She stood staring past his shoulder as if she were a recruit and he a drill instructor. "I'm sorry."

"Sorry doesn't cut it. We've been tracking this for weeks. And you go and get yourself—shit, I don't even want to discuss this anymore. Wait here."

He strode out of the room and, to his credit, didn't slam the door. Fuck. She remained standing, going over all the punishment possibilities in her head. Worse, Rick was disappointed, and she hated when that happened. Then, for what seemed the millionth time, she went over what happened. Laskin was beating Koslov's ass on the ship. Marya and Jonathan stepped in, and they seemed to be protecting Koslov. That could mean that Koslov was in on the op with them or he wasn't, and they were keeping him in the dark. If that was the case, then maybe Laskin was in on the op. How did any of this figure into the dead Petrovs? And the Koslovs in general? And running arms? And were Laskin and Koslov even alive?

She wasn't sure. And then there was the matter of Marya. What agency was she with? Or was she totally playing everybody? This was like Alice falling into Wonderland. Nothing really made sense, but there was an inside joke with everybody but Alice. And here, Ellie totally felt like Alice.

The door opened, but it wasn't Rick.

"Hey," Wes said. "You're wanted."

"I know." She followed him across the station floor to the main office conference room where all hell was sure to break loose. Rick would try to run interference—as pissed as he was—but there was only so much he could do.

She'd been up almost the entire night, and at this point, everything felt numb.

She went in.

"Have a seat," the chief said. Shit. The big boss man. Like Rick, he tended to stay formal. Even at this hour, he was dressed in a crisp button-down and tie.

This couldn't be good. She slid into a chair at the end of the table closest to the door. Rick sat across from her, but he didn't look as mad. A woman and man Ellie didn't recognize sat on either side of him. They looked like CIA. Maybe DHS.

"So we had a bit of a glitch tonight." The chief regarded her like a dad might a daughter who'd gotten into a fender bender.

"Yes, sir," she said, meeting his gaze.

"Detective O'Donnell," the woman said. "I'm with the Department of Homeland Security. This gentleman is with the FBI. Would you mind telling us precisely what happened tonight? We will be recording this."

"I figured." No names from the spooks. That's how they were going to play this, huh? Ellie recited the chain of events again. The agents asked a few clarifying questions, but pretty much allowed her to talk. When she finished, Agent DHS nodded and interlaced her fingers on the table. She regarded Ellie for a moment before speaking.

"Detective, what I am about to tell you will not leave this room. Do you understand?"

"Yes, ma'am." She stole a glance at Rick, who sat stone-faced.

"MI6 has been investigating an international arms ring. Unfortunately, you discovered far more than was anticipated."

Ellie frowned. "You're saying that you knew about this?"

The agents exchanged a look with each other while Rick's expression was a warning to Ellie. Agent DHS turned off the recorder.

"Certain communications were not effectively relayed between departments, shall we say."

Ellie stared at her. "So what exactly is going on?"

"We're not at liberty to say. What we *can* tell you is that MI6 has the lead on this investigation. We have read your department in as necessary, but as of right now, NYPD's role in this is backup only."

In other words, the op was done.

"We are in communication with the MI6 agents you were in contact with," Agent DHS continued. "We've had to create a story in which you managed to escape but you were wounded and are recovering. How close a look did Lyev Koslov get of you?"

Ellie replayed the scene in her mind. "I was wearing a hat and had bulky clothes on. It wasn't completely dark, but he probably read me as cop and didn't place me as anything but that. He hasn't seen me at Fashion Forward."

"That you're aware of," Agent FBI said.

"Yeah, okay." She exhaled, impatient. "But we've had surveillance all over that place and Koslov hasn't shown up since I started there. He may have gotten a look at me at a dance club last week, but again, it was a dance club. Different context, and I doubt he connected that sighting to me dressed like I was on the ship. But he hasn't shown up at Fashion Forward," she repeated.

Agent FBI looked at Rick.

"That's affirmative," he said. "We've had eyes on Koslov the entire time Detective O'Donnell was on site. He did not go to Fashion Forward and has not been in the vicinity."

"Thank you, Lieutenant." Agent FBI nodded at Rick. "Detective, that will be all."

Ellie looked at the captain for confirmation, and he nodded. She left and went back to her desk.

"How'd it go?" Wes asked from his desk.

"Don't know. Feds."

"Shit." He came over and gave her shoulder a squeeze. "For what it's worth, O'Donnell, it took some brass balls, boarding that ship."

"Yeah, well, it was actually really stupid."

"There's that. Next time, bring backup." He returned to his desk, and Ellie sat staring at her computer.

"O'Donnell," Rick said, but he didn't sound as mad.

She got up and went back into the conference room. The agents were gone.

The chief looked at her. "I'm reprimanding you," he said. "You did not follow procedure, and you disobeyed your team leader."

Ellie's stomach burned. "Yes, sir. I'm sorry, sir."

"That said, you've done some damn good work on this case, and it's not your fault that 'communications were not effectively relayed,'" he said in an imitation of Agent DHS's tone. "You made the model connection. MI6 hadn't been able to figure out how other buyers were involved. They guessed information might be passed at these venues, but they hadn't been able to catch Natalie Koslov doing it. So, because we're trying to keep up appearances, finish the internship at Fashion Forward."

"Sir?"

"DHS seems to think it's the best way to go about this. Hampstead isn't going to reveal your identity to Lyev Koslov, and as Detective Wallace noted in your defense, Koslov hasn't been hanging around the building."

"What about Laskin? Doesn't he figure in this?"

He nodded. "MI6 will handle that angle. You are to simply put in your time. Surveillance will continue to monitor Lyev Koslov and, if applicable, Yuri Laskin, but the Hampsteads are no longer targets."

"Is Laskin still alive?"

Rick gave her a look.

"That's not our business," the chief said.

"Does Marya Hampstead know that you want me to stay on?"

He pursed his lips thoughtfully. "She suggested it, in consultation with DHS and the FBI. It's only a couple more weeks."

"Yes, sir." That was a weird relief, that Marya was okay with it.

"And as far as the op is concerned, you're done."

Of course she was. Ellie gritted her teeth and nodded.

"You can move out of the temporary place."

Well, that was good. She nodded again.

"Dismissed. Go home and get some sleep."

"Yes, sir." Ellie returned to her desk to get her pack. She was on her way out when she heard Rick behind her.

"Els, wait."

She did. "I'm sorry," she said before he spoke again. "I fucked up. I'm going to work really hard on not doing that again."

"I know. Come on. I'll give you a ride." He sounded like he usually did, much to her continued relief. She followed him to his car, thinking she could sleep for a week. And as she sat in Rick's car as dawn broke over the Brooklyn Bridge, the memory of Marya's kiss, brief as it was, heated her far more than the morning sun.

CHAPTER 15

"Could you do me a favor?" Khalil stood in the coffee room, looking like he was about to pass out.

"Sure," Ellie said. "What's up?"

"I think I might have a virus or something. I'm going home. I already told Tyler. But I was supposed to take a cup of coffee to Ms. H and—"

"Say no more. Been there, done that. Go home. Get some rest."

"Thanks."

He left, and she loaded a French Roast pod for Marya. It would be the first time she'd seen Ms. MI6 in over a week. The night on the *Georgios* was like a bad dream, with the exception of the kiss part.

The coffee machine finished, and Ellie removed the cup but didn't put a lid on it. Marya clearly had some kind of superpower, because any time Ellie tried to drink coffee at her desk without a lid, she was guaranteed to spill it. She carried it carefully to Marya's partially open door and knocked.

"Yes," she said, and Ellie stepped in.

"Coffee. Khalil—"

"Went home. I know." Marya smiled and took the cup from her.

Her fingers brushed against Ellie's, and chills went up her spine.

"My apologies. I've been indisposed, and this is my first morning back in the office."

"You've got a fashion empire to run. I get it."

"Among other things." She held Ellie's gaze, and it was all Ellie could do not to grab her and kiss her into next week. Which would be a very bad idea given the whole MI6 thing and operation Find the Guns. And her reprimand.

"I was wondering..." Marya said, "and I know this is short notice, but is there any chance you might want to go to a party tonight? Since it's your last Friday with us." She lifted the cup to her lips and sipped. Ellie wrenched her gaze back to Marya's eyes, which didn't stop the heat building behind her ribs.

"Sure. When and where?"

"If you come to dinner with us, we'll drive you to the party."

"Is that your idea of blackmail?"

Marya smiled again. "Of course not. I'm incentivizing."

"Well, in that case, it worked. Yes. I'll go to dinner, too."

"Good. We'll be gathering in the lobby at five."

"All right." She turned to go before she said things that could get her in trouble.

"Thanks for the coffee," Marya said.

"You're welcome."

"Oh, and Ellie—I do hope you're planning on accessorizing, like you did the other night. Certain accessories come in handy, in virtually any situation."

She nodded. "Always."

"I like a woman who's prepared for anything. Because you never know what could happen."

Ellie shrugged and smiled. "I try. See you soon." She left, tingling in places she wished she wasn't. Now, all she'd be doing for the next three hours would be looking forward to being in the same room with the unattainable Marya Hampstead, who wanted her to be armed at this party. That left her something to think about, but Tyler loaded her up with some correspondence to deal with and a few things to proofread, and by the time she finished everything, it was almost five.

"Bye," Liz said as she gathered her things.

"Yeah. Have a good weekend." Ellie waited for her to leave before she called Rick and told him she was going to a fashionista dinner and party. Keeping up appearances and all. Good thing she'd taken to wearing a holster tee under her work shirts. She grabbed her bag and jacket and went to the lobby.

Ellie sipped her Coke and watched the party interactions. Dinner had been fun, because she sat next to Tyler and another guy she liked, and they talked about things other than fashion. The party, however, was a different scene entirely. People peeled off into various cliques, though Marya moved seamlessly from group to group. Clearly a woman of many talents, and not for the first time, Ellie wondered how much of her past was complete fabrication, and how exactly an MI6 agent had come to be a fashion mogul. That was years in the making, that kind of elaborate identity building.

She checked the rest of the crowd again. A few she recognized from the fashion show after-party, and some may have been in recent news reports she'd perused while researching. This party took place in a refurbished warehouse in Chelsea. She liked the exposed brick and high ceilings, which made an event like this feel more down-to-earth.

A server approached her, carrying a tray. "Would you like a refill?"

"Not right now, thanks." She set her glass on his tray and looked around the room. Lyev Koslov had arrived. And, in typical Koslov fashion, he was dressed in a well-tailored black suit. Plus, he was surrounded by women. What was the deal with this guy? Did he not know about Marya's other identity? Or was he in on this whole thing? Maybe he was Russian law enforcement? Playboy was another good cover story, if that was his situation.

Koslov took a glass of champagne from a server and toasted the women, in total party boy mode. Another man joined the group, this one in a well-fitted brown suit. Ellie watched him. Something about him was off. For one thing, he didn't fit with this jet set crowd. He looked sort of like somebody's bodyguard, and he made Koslov really nervous. The new guy leaned in and said something to Koslov. Whatever it was, Koslov's jaw clenched. The new guy gave Koslov a hard stare then walked away. Koslov watched him for a moment and then slipped back into his charming persona with the ladies.

Ellie followed Brown Suit. This party wasn't exclusive, so he'd probably just walked in. But if he had been looking specifically for Koslov, then that meant he'd been following Koslov, and that could be a problem.

Brown Suit stepped outside and lit a cigarette. Ellie watched him through the front window, made slightly difficult because it was dark out and the interior lighting caused a reflection. She followed him into the cool night air and checked her phone. The guy took a few drags then made a call. He said a few things in Russian then hung up. Ellie pretended she was talking on her own phone. He ignored her and continued to smoke until he was done with his cigarette. He tossed it carelessly onto the sidewalk, still smoldering.

A big gray SUV pulled up to the curb, and two guys got out. Clearly, they all shopped at the same clothing store—Mobsters R Us—as Brown Suit, who greeted them in Russian. The second guy, who exited the SUV glanced at Ellie, and she had to catch herself to keep from staring at him. Laskin. What the hell? She turned slightly away so he couldn't see her face.

The SUV pulled away, and the three men spoke in quiet voices in front of the party venue. She pretended to finish her call and went back inside, keeping her face averted. She had to find Marya before the Russians did, and she unfastened the top three buttons on her blouse to allow easier access to her pistol, just in case.

She scanned the crowd, but didn't see either Marya or Koslov. Not a big deal. There were lots of people here, after all. After another few moments, she had a bad feeling. Koslov was a big guy, easy to pick out, and he wasn't anywhere in sight. Bathrooms? Ellie made her way to the back and checked the women's room. Marya wasn't inside. She then checked the men's room, much to the consternation of two guys at the urinals. The stalls were not in use.

This didn't feel right at all. Back exit, then. She moved quickly down the corridor away from the bathrooms, and at the back door, she pulled her gun out, took a deep breath, and pushed the door open just enough to scan the parking area. She pushed it open a little wider and saw Koslov in the far corner, pushing Marya toward a vehicle. Quickly and quietly, she slipped through the door and hurried after them, keeping low and using the other cars as cover.

As she got closer, she heard Koslov speaking in Russian, and he didn't sound happy. He had a gun trained on Marya, and he gestured with his other hand at the passenger door of a sports car. As she got in, Koslov said something else to her, and she worked her way into the driver's seat. Ellie was now at the next car.

Now or never.

She was practically crawling as she darted behind the sports car and paused as Koslov started to get in. He had to duck to do it, and that's when Ellie made her move.

"NYPD. Freeze," she said behind him, keeping a couple of steps between them.

He did.

"Drop your weapon and step out of the vehicle." He carefully set his gun on the ground. Ellie took a step and kicked it away. "Out of the vehicle and on your knees."

He didn't move.

"Last chance."

He didn't say anything, and for a big guy, he moved fast. Ellie managed to dodge and fire at him when he lunged, but she was off balance and the shot went wide. She fell to one knee, and it was like slow motion, watching him wind up for a wicked roundhouse kick aimed at her head. Oh, hell, no. He was not going to pull Russian ninja shit on her. She threw herself backward, and his kick just missed. A blur of movement passed in front of her, and Marya decked him with a perfect punch to the side of his head. He went down hard next to the car and stayed there.

Marya offered her hand, and Ellie let her pull her up.

"Well done."

Ellie started to reply but a gray SUV pulled into the parking area and stopped in front of the sports car. Laskin got out of the passenger side, and Ellie started to raise her gun, but Marya's hand on her forearm stopped her.

"Stand down. They're with us."

What the hell? Laskin was part of the MI6 op?

Marya addressed Laskin in Russian, and he nodded and pulled a pair of cuffs out of his suit pocket. Koslov moaned and mumbled something as Laskin positioned his hands behind him and snapped the cuffs on. The two other Russian guys from earlier got out of the vehicle and hauled Koslov to his feet.

"You bitch," he said, glaring at Marya.

Laskin said something to him in Russian and Koslov stared at him. "You're dead," he said in English, eyes wide. "She shot you on the ship."

Ellie gaped at Laskin.

He shrugged. "She missed." And then he smiled, like a predator might right before it ate you. "On purpose." He pulled out a black billfold and flashed a badge at Koslov.

This looked like serious undercover Russian shit. Koslov stared first at it, then at him.

"I recommend, Lyev, that you go quietly," Marya said.

"You sold me out?" Lyev's gaze bounced from her to Laskin. "How much did they pay you? What kind of deal did you make?"

Laskin said something else in Russian, and one of the other guys took Lyev's arm while his unnamed buddy took a position on the other side. They hauled him toward the SUV, and Laskin nodded at Marya, then turned to Ellie.

"It took a while for my knee to heal," he said.

"Yeah, well, next time let me know you're one of the good guys. Or at least not a bad guy."

He smiled again, but it was genuine this time. He said something in Russian to Marya, and she nodded, but he was already on his way back to the SUV. It was gone within a few moments. If nothing else, Russians were efficient with this undercover crap. She stood with Marya, staring after the vehicle. Marya glanced at her. "Thank you."

"What just happened? Besides a major party foul?" She brushed off her trousers and put her gun away.

Marya laughed.

"For real. Does Koslov know about your other identity?"

"Not yet. And this is a discussion for another time. Champagne?"

"Love some." She followed Marya back inside and a few moments later, Marya handed her a glass.

"Care to tell me what happened at some point?" Ellie asked. "Or is this a need-to-know kind of thing? Because I did discharge my weapon, and I will have to make a report."

"I'll call to expedite the process."

"Thanks, but I'm pretty sure Rick's not going to be happy about it. Paperwork, after all."

"But in the service of national security. Cheers." She tapped her glass against Ellie's. "And thank you again."

"Sure." But she wondered if Marya had really needed her help. She was probably trained in all kinds of fight styles and could probably go mixed martial arts on somebody like Koslov without messing up her hair, even in close quarters like a sports car.

Several groupies approached and engulfed Marya, clearly starstruck. Ellie took the cue and finished her champagne with only a slight grimace. "Good night," she said to Marya. "See you later."

"Yes, you will. Good night." She gave her one of her mysterious smiles, and Ellie left before she burst into flames. She caught a train, glad to beat what looked like impending rain, and she thought about Koslov and about how Marya—probably MI6 in general—had set him up. And Laskin was clearly not the Petrov killer. Did that mean Koslov was the actual Petrov killer in addition to probably running the arms ring? And did she even care? This kind of international intrigue made her head feel like it was going to explode.

The train slowed as it approached her stop. She stepped off and went up the grimy steps to the street, wet with newly fallen rain. She picked up her pace, a hot shower foremost on her mind.

CHAPTER 16

"So Laskin is actually law enforcement?" Ellie opened another candy. "And all that crazy info on Interpol is planted?"

"Looks that way. The info's gone, now." Rick got up and went to the printer.

"That's just creepy." And maybe all those conspiracy theorists had a point, about governments knowing too much and planting info everywhere.

"The good news is, there will be no inquiry into firing your weapon at Lyev Koslov. MI6 is backing you one hundred percent." He handed her one of the papers that he had just printed. "This'll be going into your file."

She skimmed it, relieved to see in writing what he had just said. Thank you, Marya.

"Did you really save Hampstead's ass?" he asked.

"I don't really know. Maybe I helped facilitate a little. But she is seriously the female version of James Bond." She handed the paper back. "Think about it. Mysterious agent who moonlights as a celebrity fashion mogul. How the hell do you even do that? That's a cover-up for the ages. Like, years. Maybe decades."

"Maybe not as hard to do as you think, since Jonathan is MI6, too." Rick picked up his coffee. "He could've started creating the record long before she was even old enough to pick up a gun."

"Agent grooming? That's just fucked up."

He shrugged and sipped. "Weirder things have happened."

She thought about Marya kissing her on the tugboat and silently agreed with him.

"So, your last day at Fashion Forward is Tuesday. Think they'll throw you a party?" He grinned.

"Nah. Maybe drinks or lunch or something. And last night was party enough for a while."

"Maybe it's time for a vacation, Els. Seriously. When was the last time you had one?"

She didn't respond right away because she couldn't quite remember.

"See that? You don't even know. It's time."

"Maybe. Where should I go?"

"You could start with dancing tonight. It's Saturday, after all. And I heard Sue might want a date." He tried to sound innocent.

She side-eyed him. "Shut up."

"She said you're a hell of a kisser."

Ellie almost choked on her candy. "What the fuck?"

He laughed. "All part of the op, right, Els? Can't blame you, though. Sue's attractive."

"Oh, for—"

"Could've happened to anyone, having to plant one on somebody in a bar."

She knew she was blushing, which only made him laugh harder. "Sue's a good sport," Ellie muttered.

"So, apparently, are you."

"National security, bro." She glared at him and turned back to her screen. "So did Koslov kill all those Petrovs?"

Rick wiped his eyes. "All right, all right. I'll quit." He cleared his throat. "It seems that he did. MI6 has been infiltrating his operation for almost two years. He was using models, as you figured out, and so were the Petrovs, on their own circuit. Koslov was trying to wipe out some of the competition, but he didn't play it quite right, because it caused problems here. Daddy Koslov didn't know baby son Lyev was dirty-dealing, and from what I can tell, MI6 believes him."

"Do you?"

He shrugged. "He's a wily old fox, that guy. And totally capable of throwing a son under the bus."

"Where does Laskin fit in?"

"From what info MI6 shared, this arms ring was potential trouble for the Kremlin, given events in Ukraine and the fact that the guns seemed to be coming out of Russia. The last thing Putin needed was a tie to gun-running in countries that harbor terrorists. Laskin is a long-time agent, former KGB, with a long track record in this kind of stuff."

Ellie chewed the last little bit of candy. "And I'll bet Laskin isn't his real name."

"I wouldn't take that bet, because you're right. I don't know what it is, but ultimately, it probably doesn't matter." He gave her a quizzical look. "So is Hampstead going to wish you happy trails on your last day?"

"Don't know." And maybe it stung a little, that this was it for Hampstead, since Ellie had no reason to hang out at

Fashion Forward after this. Unless Gwen invited her to a fundraiser down the line that Marya happened to attend.

"On the plus side, you have a contact with MI6."

"Yeah. I guess." She really wanted to think about something else.

"Anyway, want to grab a beer?"

"Yeah." She logged out of her computer.

"And maybe you should think about that vacation. In all seriousness. This was a crazy op, and it would do you some good to chill for a while."

"I'll think about it." Not a bad idea. She should dust off her passport, maybe.

"You have tons of time accrued."

"Yeah, yeah. Put your money where your mouth is and buy me a beer."

He grinned, reached into his desk drawer, and tossed something at her. "I figured you were running out," he said when she caught the bag of candy.

"You're enabling me."

He shrugged. "Hell, if it gets work done the way you did it this past month, I'll enable the shit out of you."

She smiled and followed him out of the station.

Ellie stretched out on her couch with a sigh of relief, wearing her favorite baggy sweats. The radiator clinked and hissed in the corner and what looked like a ridiculously bad monster movie was on TV. The microwave dinged in the kitchen, and she went to retrieve her popcorn, which she dumped into a big plastic bowl before she added a few spices to it. She rinsed a coffee cup out and poured a bit of Jack Daniel's into it and sipped, deciding to top off the two beers she'd had with Rick a few hours ago.

This right here was the best kind of accessorizing, she thought as she plopped back down on the couch and prepared to stream a different movie. It was also the perfect way to forget about a super-hot woman whose day job was actually secret agent but who moonlighted as a fashion celebrity. She had thought there might be a possibility for at least a one-night stand, but it didn't seem that was in the cards. And it felt weird to contact Marya at Fashion Forward and ask her out. Kind of like invading her space, somehow.

Oh, well.

She reached for one of her remotes when her phone buzzed with a text from a number she didn't recognize. Who the hell was texting her at eleven at night? *Want some company?*

"Fuck, no," she muttered as she responded. *Wrong number. Drunk text somebody else.* She scooped up a handful of popcorn and picked up the remote when her phone buzzed again.

"Really?" Ellie muttered and debated turning her phone off, but curiosity got the better of her and she read the message.

I only had one glass of wine at dinner, Ellie. Another message followed: *So about that company...*

She stared at it. Marya? This just got interesting. *Depends on whose.* She waited for a response, almost holding her breath.

Mine.

That's doable. She was fully aware of all the meanings that could have. *When?*

Open your door.

She re-read the message a few times, and then she was off the couch and in her bedroom within seconds, where she grabbed her gun. Now ready, she went to the front door, wincing as the wooden floor creaked under her weight. Given the crazy spy movie shit of the past few days, she didn't put her eye to the peephole right away. After all, there might be some Russian model who was part of an international arms ring on the other side, with the barrel of a pistol pressed against it, pretending to be Marya.

"Who is it?"

"Your not-drunk texter," said an all-too-familiar voice on the other side of the door.

Ellie cautiously checked the peephole. Definitely Marya. No Russian models moonlighting in international arms rings in sight. She unlocked the door and opened it a little. "So. Just driving through the neighborhood? Thought you might drop by?"

"Something like that."

Ellie nodded, as if thinking. "Do you like popcorn?"

"Love it."

Ellie nodded again and swung the door open. And holy Christ on a windmill, Marya could wear anything and look good, even when it was damp from the rain. She had on jeans, sneakers, and a sweatshirt under a jean jacket. She was also wearing a baseball cap, and she looked edible even like this, and not at all like a fashion queen.

Marya smiled. "Shouldn't there be a test?"

"That was it."

"A woman of refinement. I appreciate that."

"I take my popcorn very seriously," she said as Marya stepped inside and waited while she locked up again. She smelled like rain and a hint of cologne—something crisp and clean. "Make yourself at home," Ellie said. "I'll just go put my accessory away."

"And a fine one it is." Her voice was like a caress down Ellie's back and hello, what did she think she was doing, letting Marya Hampstead, fashion empress and badass agent, into her apartment?

She returned her gun to its lockbox, but stood for a moment, a hundred different thoughts running through her head. Hell, she knew exactly why she'd let her in.

"This is really good popcorn."

She looked up. Marya stood in the doorway to her bedroom with the popcorn bowl, munching away. She had taken her jacket and cap off and she could have passed as a college co-ed spending an evening with a study group.

"Told you. Popcorn is serious business in my life."

"And you have a very nice place. It's comfortable. Feels homey."

"Thanks. Want something to drink? Soda? Mineral water? Something stronger?" Ellie brushed past her, needing to keep some distance between them until she figured out exactly what this visit was about. She picked up her cup of Jack Daniel's on the way to the kitchen.

"The second."

She went to the kitchen, and Marya followed her, still carrying the popcorn, and watched as Ellie took a bottle of sparkling water out of the fridge and poured a glass.

Marya took a drink. "Thanks."

"Sure," she said as she sipped from her cup. "And I probably don't want to know how you got my address."

"Probably not." She set her glass on the counter.

"And I'm pretty sure that wasn't your personal phone you were using."

Marya pulled a cheap flip phone out of her pocket and set it next to the glass. "Right again."

"I figured." She took another swallow from her cup and grabbed a couple pieces of popcorn. "And I'm guessing you're not here for a debriefing."

"Depends on whose briefs."

Ellie almost choked on the liquor, which made Marya laugh. "Walked right into that. Okay, maybe you're here because you heard about my popcorn skills."

"Could be. Or maybe I'm wondering about your other skills." And Marya grabbed the front of Ellie's sweatshirt and pulled her close. She moved her lips slowly but oh, so deliciously against Ellie's, the popcorn bowl between them preventing closer contact, but it was kind of cute, like they were teenagers, tentatively exploring.

Marya's fingers traced the line of Ellie's jaw as her kiss became more insistent, and there wasn't any part of Ellie's anatomy that wasn't on fire, wasn't any part of her that didn't ache at the feel of Marya's tongue on her lips.

Ellie extricated the popcorn bowl from between them and managed to put it on the counter, along with her cup, and then there was nothing but clothing between them as she pulled her close. She was sure there was nothing on earth that felt as good as Marya Hampstead's mouth.

Unless it was Marya Hampstead's hands in her hair. And oh, God, on her neck. Then her back—

"I thought you had a policy," Ellie said between kisses.

"I do." She lightly bit Ellie's lip.

"You're kind of violating it right now." She nipped Marya's lip right back.

"Mmm. Technically, no." She worked her hands down Ellie's back to her hips.

Ellie kissed her hard and deep then pulled away just enough that their mouths barely touched. "How's that?"

"Your last day is the day after tomorrow, and I won't be in the office, so we won't have to deal with the fallout from an office affair."

"Seriously? That's your justification?"

"How about this? You weren't really an intern."

"That's weak, Marya." She smiled and kissed her again, but Marya had slightly different ideas, because she pulled away and moved her mouth along Ellie's jaw, and her breath was hot near her ear.

"Say it again," she whispered.

"What?"

"My name."

Ellie cupped Marya's face in her hands and fell into the depths of her eyes, like she had the first time she'd seen them. "Marya," she said, "I'm going to ignore your policy." She ran her lips across Marya's, and was rewarded with a soft groan. "In fact, I'm going to ignore it really hard."

"God, yes."

A million sparks shot down her spine, and she moved her hands to Marya's hips and nuzzled her neck. Marya's fingers digging into her shoulders only stoked a fire she'd been patiently tending for weeks, and Ellie backed her against the counter to kiss her like her life depended on it. She tasted like popcorn and secrets, and somewhere in the back of Ellie's mind a warning flashed.

Yes, this was hotter than she could have ever imagined, but it couldn't end well. She's a goddamn agent. And fashion celebrity. There is no chance this will go anywhere.

So what? Ellie moved her hands under Marya's sweatshirt and tee, and oh, God, the way her skin felt. The ice queen was anything but. Her skin was warm and smooth beneath her palms, and Marya moaned and sucked on Ellie's lip.

The warning flashed again. This is definitely not going to end well.

Oh, yes it is, Ellie argued with herself. It was going to end amazingly well, and she didn't care that it was a one-night stand. It was so worth it, especially now that Marya's hands were underneath her sweatshirt, and then suddenly neither of them was wearing a sweatshirt and somehow they were moving, stumbling out of the kitchen between kisses into the living room, then toward the bedroom. They didn't get that far.

Ellie pushed her against the wall, a hand braced on either side of her head, and they stared at each other, chests heaving. She ran her fingers along Marya's shoulder holster. "I like a woman in leather."

"Lucky for me." She reached for the buckle but Ellie stopped her.

"I'll work around it." She slowly unbuttoned Marya's jeans, using her body to keep her pinned against the wall as she did it, the butt of Marya's pistol digging into her chest. So hot. She adjusted her position, lips hovering very close to Marya's mouth.

"Yes," she said, breathy, and Ellie kissed her deep, all the pent-up longing of the past few weeks surging through her as she worked one hand down the front of Marya's jeans and cupped her, the damp heat on her fingers making her burn even hotter.

"You've had this on your mind for a while, haven't you?" Ellie gently stroked, her hand still on the outside of Marya's panties.

"You have no idea," came the response in muted gasps.

"Tell me," she whispered, then added, "Marya."

The answering moan sent a wave of heat down her thighs. She kept stroking, and Marya's hands were all over her back and neck, and oh, God, but she moved so well.

"The first time you brought me coffee. You weren't intimidated."

Ellie stopped stroking her, and Marya made a small, sad noise in the back of her throat.

"I don't give a shit about the celebrity side of you. I want to make that clear."

Marya met her gaze and held it like it might be breakable. "I know."

"And I probably don't care about the agent side, either. Though I will admit I have a thing for badass women."

She smiled. "Same here." She ran her fingertips down Ellie's cheek and let them linger on her chin. "You were an anomaly at Fashion Forward."

Something in her tone—Ellie groaned. "You knew. Fuck, you knew way before the *Georgios*. And here I thought I'd rocked that role."

She laughed, a rich, velvety sound that wrapped around her like silk sheets. "You did rock it. I wasn't sure until the club."

"Shit. Your dad?"

"Partially. Otherwise, it just didn't make sense for you to show up there. Too much of a coincidence. On the other hand, I figured you were law enforcement, which meant you probably weren't actually interested in a long-term career in the fashion industry. That allowed me to be a little more expressive about certain things." And she kissed her into next week, kissed her maybe into the middle of next month. At least that's what it felt like. And then, sadly, she stopped.

"I've been MI6 a long time. And it took me a while to figure out who you were. Which means you did, as you put it, rock that role."

"Yeah, about that. How is it you're that and a fashion celebrity? How does that even work?"

"Long story."

"Maybe you'll tell me some day."

She smiled. "Maybe."

And Ellie got lost again in her eyes, and nothing past that mattered. "Whatever. Right now, I don't think I care." She started stroking again, and Marya sighed, a sweet, longing sound. She buried her fingers in Ellie's hair and thrust slowly against her hand.

"I'm going to ignore your policy right here, right now," Ellie said, and she unzipped Marya's jeans and slipped her hand down her underwear and their groans matched when her fingertips glided through heat and moisture.

"Please," Marya said, her teeth clenched. "God, please."

But Ellie teased her. She slid her fingers in only to withdraw them seconds later, and continue stroking, matching her pace, losing herself to deep, hot kisses and the feel of Marya's tongue in her mouth and on her lips.

Finally, Ellie slid in and nothing felt this good. Oh, God. This time she stayed, thrusting gently at first, then a little harder, and every motion of her hand made her ache even more. "Tell me, Marya," she said against her lips. "Tell me what you want."

"What you're doing now is exactly what I want," she managed. "Now tell me when exactly you wanted me."

"It would have to be when I brought you coffee the first time."

Marya groaned, and her fingers dug into Ellie's skin, beneath her T-shirt, and then her hands, warm and strong, were on her stomach. They slid up and cupped her breasts, and all kinds of heat roiled through her chest and down her thighs.

"You weren't wearing your sunglasses," Ellie managed to say as she plunged in harder and faster. "I'm kind of an eye woman, too."

"That's all it took?" she was panting, and she suddenly pulled her close, her hands on her back, now.

"You underestimate the power of your eyes." She slid her other hand under Marya's thigh and lifted it, holding it while she thrust in and out. God, she was so turned on she'd probably come, too.

"Harder," she said between gasps, and Ellie obliged, and then Marya was exploding around her hand, thrusting hard against her, head thrown back against the wall, a fierce grin stretching her lips wide. Ellie may have had an out-of-body experience, watching her release. Within moments, Marya was kissing her again, as Ellie unbuckled her holster and lowered it carefully to the floor while maintaining their position against the wall.

"The safety's on," Marya said as she pulled her T-shirt off, amused.

"I know. Just taking care of good equipment."

"Something you clearly know how to do well," she said as she slipped her hand inside Ellie's sweat pants. "Mmm," she practically purred when her fingers trailed lightly over her soaked underwear. "What do you want?" she said, breath hot against Ellie's ear.

"You," Ellie said with a groan. "All over me."

"Easily arranged." She took Ellie's T-shirt off and spent long, delicious moments kissing her shoulders, neck, and chest in time with the strokes of her fingers. Ellie removed Marya's bra and let it slip to the floor. Marya unfastened hers in turn, and as it fell, she pulled Ellie close. The warmth of her chest and breasts on her skin made her shudder.

"Hold on," Marya whispered before she slid down Ellie's body until she was on her knees, back still to the wall.

What—Oh, Jesus. She pulled Ellie's pants down past her hips and then did the same with her underwear, only much slower. Ellie braced herself on the wall with both hands as Marya teased her with fingers and tongue until she was breathing like she'd just run a marathon.

Stars. She was seeing stars, arms and shoulders trembling from pleasure and pain as they worked to keep her braced on the wall as Marya coaxed her right to the edge of orgasm, kept her there for a few excruciating seconds, then gently pushed her over. Stars, planets, comets... She was pretty sure she saw them all as she came. She was also pretty sure she was going to collapse, but Marya was suddenly standing, and her arms were wrapped around her, allowing her to sag against her.

"I really like ignoring your policy."

Marya chuckled. "Me, too."

Ellie kissed her, and just like that, she was ready to go another few rounds, her taste on Marya's lips and tongue, their damp, warm skin pressed close. "I could do this all night," she said, but that was an understatement. All week. Hell, all month.

"Good. Because I'm now taking you to bed." The look in Marya's eyes made Ellie ache all over again, and she let herself be pulled to the bedroom.

CHAPTER 17

Ellie rolled over, but the bed was empty. That was a bummer. MI6 agents were quiet when they left. She sighed and opened her eyes in the morning light and stared at the ceiling for a few moments. Delicious memories of her time with Marya made her tingle. She'd gotten her one-night stand.

Unfortunately, she wanted another one. And maybe another one after that. She frowned, because she heard soft music and smelled coffee, and both seemed to be in her apartment. She sat up just as Marya appeared in the doorway, wearing Ellie's clothes and carrying a cup of coffee. It was strangely endearing.

"Morning." She smiled, sat carefully on the bed, and leaned in for a kiss. She tasted like cinnamon candy, and Ellie laughed against her lips.

"Found my stash, huh?"

Marya smiled and handed her the cup. "Right next to the coffee filters. You need to work on hiding things better."

"I'm not trying to hide those things." She sipped. "So I guess you're not needed anywhere?"

"I'm in London." She smiled again.

"Of course you are. Like you were in Boston the night of the *Georgios*."

"Exactly." She ran her fingertip down Ellie's cheek. "I do have to make the London rumor true this evening, though, and I'll be spending a lot of time in the London office during the next quarter. While things with the op settle."

"So how does an MI6 agent become a fashion mag executive?" She handed the cup back.

"My mother had connections while I was growing up, and both my parents thought it might offer an interesting cover."

"So you were agent first, *then* fashion exec?"

Marya nodded and sipped. "I had always wanted to be an agent, like my father, and my long-suffering mother reluctantly agreed. She came up with the fashion cover story, actually, and glamour can be fun, so I worked my way up through the industry using a combination of my own attitude and skills and my mother's connections. But I also surround myself with lots of people who know what they're doing. It's all about illusion in this line of work. As you know." She kissed her again, long, lingering, almost tender. "And you?"

"I'm an anomaly."

Marya laughed. "I know. Does that mean nobody in your family is law enforcement?" She handed her the cup.

"Besides me, nope."

"So what happened?"

"Too many comics and crime shows as a kid. I wasn't really interested in the military, so I just went the criminology and criminal justice route, but I seemed to have a talent for research and finding connections that others miss."

"I noticed."

"I do all right in the field, too." Ellie smiled and sipped.

"I noticed that, too."

They were quiet for a while, and Ellie fell again into Marya's eyes. "You're not at all like your public persona," she said.

"Good. Otherwise, I doubt I'd be here."

"True. I wouldn't have let you in because I don't think your public persona is the kind of woman who likes popcorn."

"No, she's not." Marya smiled. "But this one is. And this one also really likes breakfast."

"I like you a bit more for that. There's a diner around the corner, and I doubt they'll know who you are."

"Excellent." She took Ellie's sweats off, sadly, and pulled her jeans on. "I have to be at the airport by four today."

"How long will you be in London?" Ellie got out of bed and grabbed a pair of jeans out of her hamper, and it dawned on her, that a question like that might put inappropriate expectations on whatever this was. "I mean—for conversation's sake," she amended. "And you don't have to answer that, actually, if you don't want to." She put on a clean T-shirt and sweatshirt, knowing full well she smelled like one hell of a great night. She holstered her gun at the small of her back.

"I'll be there a while."

She looked over at Marya, who was buckling her own holster.

"But I was wondering if you had some time in the near future. Maybe you'd be interested in an overseas trip?" She sounded hopeful.

Ellie stared at her. "Are you asking me on a date?"

She grinned. "Yes. An unconventional, distant date, but a date nonetheless."

"I'm in. Tell me when and where."

"Two weeks?"

"Done. I'll put in for the time off. Rick's been after me to take a break."

"He's a wise man." Marya put her sweatshirt and baseball cap on. "Can you give me a day you'll start your vacation?"

"How about two weeks from this Friday?"

"I'll clear my calendar."

"Where should I meet you?" Ellie put on her sneakers.

"I'll let you know."

Ellie looked at her, and Marya laughed. "Trust me," she said and kissed her into next year, easily. "Now, breakfast. And more stories, I hope."

"What about you?"

She held Ellie's gaze, questioning.

"Which Marya am I getting once we leave?"

"This one."

Ellie waited.

"No celebrities," she assured her. "No agents. Maybe stories about them, though."

"All right, then. Not that there's anything wrong with celebrities or agents. It's just that I kind of prefer this Marya's company."

"I prefer being this Marya around you."

"Good to know." And she kissed her. So it was going to be a bit more than a one-night stand. She was fine with that. More than fine. Beyond their next meeting, she couldn't say, but for right now, things were exactly where they needed to be.

"Mexico."

Ellie looked over at Rick, puzzled. "What?"

"You're going to Mexico, right?"

She rolled her eyes. "I haven't decided yet." She focused on her computer again.

"Your time off starts this Friday—three days—and you still don't know what you want to do or where you want to go? How about Puerto Rico? Easy flight down there from here. And you could probably get one cheap, even this late."

"Dude, I told you, I haven't decided. I might road trip to visit my mom or something." Wes laughed on the other side of the room and tossed a pen at somebody. Rick's desk phone rang, but he ignored it.

"Come *on*, Els. Do something spectacular. Out of the ordinary. Go to France. Pick up some French woman."

She laughed. She *was* actually going to fly overseas and pick up a woman. But she wasn't about to tell him that now. "That sounds like projection, bro. Maybe you need to take some time off and do that. Go find your Queen Bey in Paris."

"You're killin' me, here, O'Donnell."

"You'll be fine." She ate a candy and took a drink of coffee and thought of Marya, and how they'd spent part of that amazing Sunday in bed, and how they'd made more coffee and laughed and talked before ending up on the couch doing a lot more than talking. Marya had lingered until the last possible minute, and Ellie's lips still tingled at the memories. She ached and burned in the best possible ways.

Rick finally answered his desk phone, and Ellie finished a report, trying not to think about how Marya felt naked against her. A flush raced up her thighs, and she took another drink of coffee, as if that would somehow help. Her desk phone rang. She didn't recognize the number, but it was a local area code.

"O'Donnell," she answered.

"Hi," said a very familiar voice. "You need to go to the Pig and Pint this evening and pick something up."

She smiled. Marya always got right to the point. "Okay. Will do. Anything else?" She could feel Rick's gaze on her, and she glared at him.

"Yes. But it involves things I'd rather show you in a few days."

"Sounds good. Talk to you later."

"Definitely." She hung up, and Ellie returned the phone to its cradle.

"That wasn't a business call," Rick said.

"Yes, it was. *My* business."

"Date call," he said, beaming. "On your work phone? Who is it?"

"Oh, for Christ's sake. Gwen's having some people over, and I decided to go."

"She wouldn't call you on your work phone."

"Whatever."

"I'll find out," he said. "I always do." And he grinned.

"Give it a rest. I'm having drinks with Gwen." At least, she probably would, at some point in the future. After she took care of this overseas booty call.

"You met somebody at Fashion Forward," he pressed. "And you didn't want to give your cell phone out because she might be crazy."

"Yes. That's it. I'm going on a date with a potential nutjob, but she's hot enough that I can overlook the crazy for a night."

He laughed. "Nothing wrong with a one-nighter. And good for you. She's more available than Morales, right?"

"Shut up."

His desk phone rang again before he could tease any more, and Ellie pointedly put her earbuds in, giving him an extra glare, though they both knew she didn't mean it. Besides, in two hours, she'd be on her way to the Pig and Pint. She pulled up another report.

Only two tables were full when she entered, but that was to be expected, since it wasn't even three o'clock yet. Ellie chose a small table in the back and settled in.

"Hi, there. Good to see you again." The same server from the last time Ellie was here approached with a glass of what looked like whiskey, a menu, and a manila envelope. She put all three on the table. "How are you?"

"Good. You?"

"Excellent. Let me know when you're ready to order some food." She winked and went back to the bar.

Ellie picked up the glass first and sipped. Red Breast. She smiled and picked up the envelope, one of those padded jobs. Something in it made it bulge. She opened it and took out a note, what looked like plane tickets, and a flip phone.

She looked at the tickets first and her eyes widened. Athens, Greece, leaving this Friday. The note was written in Marya's strong, spare print, with no extraneous flourishes. "When you arrive, turn the phone on and text me." She had included a number and finished with, "No celebrities, no agents, no policies. Just us."

Oh, hell, yes. She put everything back into the envelope and scanned the menu. The server appeared a few moments after that.

"What are you in the mood for?"

Ellie smiled. All kinds of things, none of which were on the menu. "Club sandwich."

"Good choice." She took the menu. "Another drink?"

She considered. "I'll finish with a Coke."

The server nodded. "Keeping your wits about you?"

"Something like that."

"Better than the alternative." She flashed a smile and went to the kitchen.

Ellie sipped her whiskey and silently toasted internships, undercover ops, and the start of her vacation.

And maybe, just maybe, the start of something else.

About Andi Marquette

Andi Marquette is a native of New Mexico and Colorado and an award-winning mystery, science fiction, and romance writer. She also has the dubious good fortune to be an editor who spent 15 years working in publishing, a career track that sucked her in while she was completing a doctorate in history.

She is co-editor of *All You Can Eat: A Buffet of Lesbian Romance and Erotica*, a Lambda finalist, and *Order Up: A Menu of Lesbian Romance and Erotica*. Her most recent novels include the romances *The Secret of Sleepy Hollow*, *The Bureau of Holiday Affairs*, and *From the Hat Down*.

When she's not writing novels, novellas, and stories or co-editing anthologies, she serves as both an editor for *Luna Station Quarterly*, an ezine that features speculative fiction written by women and as co-admin of the popular blogsite Women and Words. When she's not doing that, well, hopefully she's managing to get a bit of sleep.

CONNECT WITH ANDI:

Website: www.andimarquette.com

OTHER BOOKS FROM YLVA PUBLISHING

www.ylva-publishing.com

The Secret of Sleepy Hollow

(Twice Told Tales. Lesbian Retellings – Book #2)

Andi Marquette

ISBN: 978-3-95533-515-1
Length: 166 pages (45,000 words)

Graduate student Abby Crane schedules a research trip over Halloween weekend for Sleepy Hollow, in search of material for her doctoral thesis and answers about her long-lost ancestor, Ichabod Crane. Local folklore says he disappeared at the hands of the ghostly headless horseman—or did he? With the help of the attractive Katie McClaren, Abby finds much more than she ever thought possible.

Requiem for Immortals

(The Law Game – Book #1)

Lee Winter

ISBN: 978-3-95533-710-0
Length: 263 pages (86,000 words)

Requiem is a brilliant cellist with a secret. The dispassionate assassin has made an art form out of killing Australia's underworld figures without a thought. One day she's hired to kill a sweet and unassuming innocent. Requiem can't work out why anyone would want her dead—and why she should even care.

Four Steps

Wendy Hudson

ISBN: 978-3-95533-690-5
Length: approx. 92,000 words

Alex Ryan lives a simple life. She has her farm in the Scottish countryside, and the self-imposed seclusion suits her until a crime that has haunted her for years tears through the calm and shatters the fragile peace she'd finally managed to find.

Lori Hunter's greatest love is the mountains. They're her escape from the constant hustle and bustle of everyday life. Growing up was neither traditional nor easy for Lori, but now she's beginning to realise she's settled for both. A dead-end relationship and little to look forward to. Her solution when the suffocation sets in? Run for the hills.

A chance encounter in the mountains of the Scottish Highlands leads Alex and Lori into a whirlwind of heartache and a fight for survival as they build a formidable bond that will be tested to its ultimate limits.

COMING FROM
YLVA PUBLISHING

www.ylva-publishing.com

The Lavender List

Meg Harrington

After the Second World War, Amelia Maldonado opts to live a quiet life bussing tables at a diner during the day and going out for auditions at night. The one bright spot is her friendship with the charming Laura Wright, a well-heeled woman with a mysterious war-related past.

When Laura shows up outside the diner barely conscious and spitting lousy lies, Amelia takes it upon herself to figure out the truth. From mobsters to spies, Amelia quickly finds herself forced back into a world of shadows she thought she'd escaped long ago and thrust into partnership with the one person she's sure can ruin her—the enigmatic Laura Wright.

If Looks Could Kill
© 2016 by Andi Marquette

ISBN: 978-3-95533-721-6

Also available as e-book.

Published by Ylva Publishing, legal entity of Ylva Verlag, e.Kfr.

Ylva Verlag, e.Kfr.
Owner: Astrid Ohletz
Am Kirschgarten 2
65830 Kriftel
Germany

www.ylva-publishing.com

First edition: 2016

Credits
Edited by Jove Belle
Cover Design by Dirt Road Design
Cover Photo by © Subbotina Anna | Dollar Photo Club
Vector Design by Freepik.com

Printed in Great Britain
by Amazon